The Glass Cottage

The Peter Redgrove Library

Other Peter Redgrove books available from Stride:

The Peter Redgrove Library:

1. *In the Country of the Skin*
2. *The Terrors of Dr. Treviles**
3. *The Glass Cottage**
4. *The God of Glass*
5. *The Sleep of the Great Hypnotist*
6. *The Beekeepers*
7. *The Facilitators*
8. *The Colour of Radio: Essays and Interviews*

[*with Penelope Shuttle]

The Laborators
Abyssophone
Orchard End
What the Black Mirror Saw
Sheen
A Singer for the Silver Goddess

A Curious Architecture [contributor]
Earth Ascending [contributor]

i.m. Peter Redgrove:
Full of Star's Dreaming: Peter Redgrove 1932-2003

The Glass Cottage

A Nautical Romance

Peter Redgrove

with Penelope Shuttle

The Glass Cottage
This edition 2006

ISBN 1-905024-10-x

Cover design by Neil Annat
Cover photos © Alistair Fitchett
Used with kind permission of the artist

The Peter Redgrove Library
is published by
Stride Publications
4b Tremayne Close
Devoran
Cornwall TR3 6QE
England

www.stridebooks.co.uk

Thanks

The Peter Redgrove Library is grateful to the following subscribers who have helped make the publication of these titles possible:

Cliff Ashcroft
Andrew Bailey
Martin Bax
Hazel Carruthers
Philip Fried
Mark Goodwin & Nikki Clayton
David Grubb
Michael Longley
Adrian & Celia Mitchell
Brian Louis Pearce
Malcolm Ritchie
Geoff Sutton & Bernard Gilhooly
Leonie Whitton & David Westby

to the following for help, encouragement and support in other ways:

Tony Frazer
Neil Roberts
Penelope Shuttle
the late Philip Hobsbaum

and to Arts Council England, South West for financial support.

Introduction

Peter liked to give himself challenges. After his father Jim died Peter set himself the bereavement challenge of following the complex three-year Prana Yama (yoga breathing) programme devised by the yoga master Iyengar. And he accomplished it, a feat accompanied by his reading of the Bible over the same three years.

The writing of *The Glass Cottage* was a similar self-tasking. In the autumn of 1974 Peter and I sailed to New York on the QE2. Peter was to teach in the English Department of Colgate University (yes, the toothpaste university) in New York State, as Visiting Chair for two semesters. Despite a sizeable teaching schedule, and plus the fact that we were both deeply engaged in researching what would become our book on menstruation, *The Wise Wound*, Peter decided to write a novel based on our voyage.

The voyage came about by accident, due to our misreading and under-estimating the cost, thinking it cheaper than flying. Discovering our mistake, Peter thought to defray these extra costs by writing *The Glass Cottage*.

He was the main author while I cheered on from the sidelines. He'd show me part of a chapter. DOES THIS WORK? NO. He'd show me part of another chapter. DOES THIS WORK? YES. And I did some final tweaking.

Opening with the ritualistic murder of a female school-teacher found dead with a Christ-like wound in her side, in which the murderer places the dead woman's gold watch, we are offered a multiplicity of suspects. One man confesses, despite being innocent. The man who committed the crime ever afterwards finds the memory of the murder sexually arousing, but he is never apprehended. Is the murderer the poet interested in menstruation, Endenberg the freckled old psychotherapist, or his sad friend Jeremy? Is he the Chief Steward, the Captain, the wry Ship's Doctor or the former patient of Jung?

I hadn't re-read *The Glass Cottage* for many years. As soon as I began reading, it was as if a door had been thrown wide open in welcome. There was Peter, telling the story. His presence surges through the novel. There's his high-voltage energy in theme and language, his unique vision seamlessly mingling psychological, philosophical and ecological insights; there are some very acute perceptions about educational establishments on both sides of the Atlantic, scatological detail, and, of course, unfailing interest and delight in sexual experience.

Like all writers who fully celebrate life, Peter was deeply concerned with death, and what becomes of us after death. There's as much darkness in *The Glass Cottage* as there is light, despite the title, which speaks of light.

Peter was fascinated by the QE2, its materiel, its rituals, its social life, its engines and its spirit. Here the QE2 appears under the explicitly emblematic name of the SS Messenger, speeding across the Atlantic 'like an inter-library loan between Good Olde English and the Universal States'.

The Glass Cottage is a message sent back to England from America about life, death, the afterlife, time, bereavement, murder, menstruation, obsession, crime, punishment, heightened states of perception, the processes of teaching; and also includes some of Peter's current favourite scientific ideas. "Do you think that electron degeneracy is the clue to short-term memory in the brain?" I shouted along the bus.

Much of the message is about homesickness, a longing especially for Boscastle, a village on the north coast of Cornwall, where Peter and I holidayed every year for thirty years. Every time we walked from the village to Minster Church we passed a cottage built close to the little river Jordan and we christened this *The Glass Cottage*, from the way its windows reflected the river light. We longed to live in that cottage! I went back to Boscastle two years after Peter's death, and again walked to Minster, passing the cottage with the stream flowing in front of it, a heap of young yellow goslings on the lawn. Boscastle is so accurately and magically personified in this book that I step through the pages and am back there with Peter. I realise other readers won't have the many personal associations that I do with Boscastle, but the achieved reality of Boscastle in Peter's writing enables any reader to be drawn into that strange compelling resonant landscape.

Many events in the novel are imaginary. Others are based on actual events. The visit down the Cornish mineshaft is true; in 1968 Peter went on such a visit. He is the awkward Jimmy who drops his safety helmet down the shaft. The exasperation the Professor feels about American furniture — 'One of the things that irritated him about America was the immense silliness of the furniture . . .' is Peter's own annoyance. The Blake specialist who finds the clitoris everywhere in Blake's poetry is based on an academic Peter met on an earlier visit to America. The student who suddenly sings a Dylan Thomas poem in a tutorial was a real student at Colgate, and the recollection of Dylan Thomas reading at Cambridge is a memory from Peter's student days.

Another mystery, besides the murder, is about the ever-changing *Spirit of the Liner*, which inhabits a different passenger each night. The professor tells us that '. . . the consciousness of the liner could at certain times every day and night afford to lose hold on the details of its functioning and instead wander, disguised as one of the passengers, through its holds, bathrooms and cabin-spaces.'

Another presiding spirit is the ghost of Sylvia Plath. Peter knew Sylvia through his friendship with Ted Hughes. The gold watch that is found in the murdered woman's wound is Plath's 'love set you going like a fat gold watch', one of her few life-affirming poems. Plath inspired the woman character who is questioned simultaneously by police on both sides of the Atlantic — one of Peter's inspired comedic passages and technically very innovative — and who shows the startled cops a wound in her side. She is also the Spirit of the Liner.

The poet interested in menstruation admonished Plath's ghost for choosing death over life. 'Did you not ask for this blood sisterhood? Is the Moon not a door?' But in the afterlife Plath has moved on, she is accompanied by a native American who is guiding her to peace. Free and untroubled now, Plath says: 'Time started when we were born, held up to our mother's ears like a "fat gold watch", and ends when we die, praises be. To take the watch out of the wound is to live and be in time, but not of it.'

This is a poet's novel: mercurial, disrespectful, inquisitive, mocking, reverent. Water is a constant factor, but we are also taken to mountain-tops and to the depths of the earth. For Peter the questions we ask of and about the world are poetry; the answers we search for and shift through are poetry. But Peter is also a beguiling and seductive storyteller. Apparently tangential in style at first glance, we read on to discover a complex implicate web of associations draw together with great skill and purpose. This is Peter's *Voyage Out*. We travel with him, entertained and enlightened by the horizon of every page.

Penelope Shuttle

'Out of life comes death and out of death life, out of the young the old, and out of the old the young, out of waking sleep, and out of sleeep waking, the stream of creation and dissolution never stops.'

Heraclitus

I played games in my mind with that boat. I called that liner, the ship of blood. Its colours were black and white, its colours to see. But I felt that its quality was the crimson of blood. This black and white vehicle with its funnels broad as garages banded in black and white, its white rails for white departing faces to lean over their black stanchions, the black and white uniforms of its stewards and stewardesses, were nevertheless in truth ambulance colours, meat-wagon colours, for its cargo was blood, flesh and blood. Its demeanour was that of a sledge across the snowy-grey sea; it was a sledge packed with meat.

I wonder whether women travelling by ship synchronize their cycles so that all menstruate together? Then it would be a great moonship, with towering sides. Nightly, it is a ship of fools. There are three bands, two playing rock and pop, and one playing genteel selections for the middle-aged, of whom there are a great many. There is a casino, like a great whirlpool in the middle of the ship, like a bath-plug down which the money pours. There is a cinema, attended by a silent dark minority. There are the cabins, very small under the water-line near the keel of the ship, growing in size and magnificence as the captain's bridge is neared. None can match in splendour the captain's quarters, and no one can reach these except by invitation. Invited, your steward must guide you along corridors that run through the liner from stem to stern, a thousand-foot length. Windowless corridors lighted by electricity and lined with honeycomb of steel cabins. The feeling there is of a great air-raid shelter. Some bomb is hovering overhead and will plunge through level after level, converting the lift-shafts to fountains of blood. Meanwhile the great shelter keeps its pattern in space of corridor and staircase, lift and swimming-pool, bureau and dance-band. Its bright lights stream over the dark sea, its bright lights keep the dark from peering in. Steel doors fit over the night and Atlantic weather outside. In the long corridors it is miles undersea, and the hum of the engines is the planet's motion.

* * *

Three thousand miles is a long journey by water. I hold you in my arms and I feel the boat rushing through the miles of salt water. I have held you in my arms as the train hurries across countryside, now I hold you balanced on a steel shelf over unimaginable depths of the sea, like one page facing another in a black and white printed book in an enormous black and white travelling library. But I do not think that such size is unimaginable. We are naked and our forces flow, I stroke you wet and enter, we are no longer in a boat but travelling within each other and we have not yet come to the end of our journey.

Afterwards you say that you saw the great cliffs of the coasts like the grandest of canyons, but the water was quite invisible, and the whole sea-bed lit up by the moon, resembling with its craters and pinnacles, the surface of that moon. Moon poring over moon. One small moonlit mote like a black and white gnat winged a solitary and unsupported course over the canyon, like a glider, a tight-rope walker. Then the stars blazed, and you lost sight of it. It is a pity, you say, that we have to use boats. If your shoes are leather, you say, the whole earth is covered with leather. Just now, our world is a black and white liner, with narrow beds. The cavernous sea-bed is metal-roofed.

* * *

She wore a long print dress of a light colour scrawled with a design that resembled large unformed letters. Her shoes were tall Japanese sandals made of wood, fastened with black tie laces. Her head was large and held straight on her neck, as a child naturally holds its head with poise. This great size of her head was emphasized by the hair-style, cut short and swept upwards. The eyes were dark and sometimes bolted sideways like a frightened hare. She sat with her fists clenched and her midriff shivering.

'I wake at four each morning screaming French,' she said. 'You told us that when we began to dream it would be better.' I asked her whether she had dreamed at all. 'I dreamed of you,' she said, 'I realized I was dreaming about you.' 'What do you mean?' 'I was simply awake and sitting at the table, then I realized you were in this great room, fussing with papers in your briefcase. I wanted to speak to you, but I couldn't. I opened my mouth but it was shivering and wouldn't talk. Then I heard a beautiful sound and I turned round. There in the window and passing through into the room were hundreds of white birds.' 'The birds were speaking for you.' 'But why did I dream about you?' 'You have elected me as a guide.' 'But why do I wake screaming in French?' 'Have you a lover?' 'Yes, he is away in France.'

* * *

The lights were on in the cabin as they so often are since our passengers pay no extra for electricity. I used my passkey and struggled in with my pail of rags and my brushes. Odd that they dress us so smartly in black and white, yet they give us such worn and ugly tools to work with. Traditional to the craft, I suppose. The lady lay on the bed, which was stripped. So was she, quite nude. Blood had run out of the cut high on her midriff, and had soaked into the sheet. My first thought was that she was asleep, then that she was as still as a photograph, then that she was bleeding and I must staunch the blood, then that she was dead. I forced myself to cross over the floor to the phone. I lacked a hand to pick it up, I got involved in a foolish way with the cord and the bucket. I dialled for the chief steward. 'Are you alone Sir, this is Molly. I'm afraid one of the customers is wasted. Yes Sir, dead. Wounded. There's no knife that I can see. Cabin 2431.' My hair, my face was soaked. I was crying and sweating. I looked in the mirror and saw the face on the bed. Black hair, white skin, red stab-wound on the bed. Black hair, white skin, white shirt, black tie, black skirt in the mirror. I unpinned the tie and opened my shirt. The wound would be just above the waistband of my skirt. I pulled the skin there, I could see no wound. I unzipped the skirt and examined my body for the wound. Then I lay on the bed with the dead lady and tried to warm her. I felt between her legs to try and warm her and bring her to life. She was cool, but not cold. Her cunt was lax and sticky. I laid my hand there and slept. This is how they found me.

* * *

The English schoolteacher travelling to her exchange job in Canada was not at dinner, nor at breakfast the next morning. The steward looked uncomfortable and said she had not been feeling well. I went down to her cabin after breakfast. It was locked and I couldn't make her hear. I stood knocking at the door and I felt a light touch on my shoulder. The stewardess, who looked not unlike my friend, asked me to go with her. I was a little worried now. As we walked along I lit a cigarette. 'Where are we going?' 'The Chief Steward.' This short and wizened officer sat in his office on One-deck. 'I'm afraid your friend has had an accident', he informed me. I could not catch his glance. I thought she had probably been taken ill and was in the ship's infirmary. 'No, she's dead. I'm very sorry to say that she was killed some time in the early evening yesterday.' I thought of the afternoon we had spent in each other's arms fucking and dreaming. The throb of the engines grew louder and a swell seemed to hit the ship, heaving the room. I saw the moon-abyss of the Atlantic she had spoken of, and saw her falling, spinning into its depths. A cold knife-blade touched my lips. The rim of the drinking-glass clicked on my teeth and the ice-water made me splutter. 'We have the criminal in the brig,' the Chief Steward resumed, 'it seems he was her lover. I must ask you not to mention this to any of the other passengers. The Lady's cabin will be sealed for police examination when we dock.'

* * *

'It may seem rather harsh to tell a Professor he cannot visit the engine-rooms,' said the Second officer, teetering over me with his gin glass in his hand, 'but I had to say this to an Admiral the other day. You see, we think if They don't know where the engines are, we're more difficult to hi-jack.' 'Is that a real possibility?' 'It wouldn't be the first time. Though not on this line, thank God.' 'I suppose mines would be set and hostages taken from among the passengers.' 'We can't have first-class passengers walking the plank. Yes, I think they would shoot a few passengers and demand money for the lives of the others. We might have to set them off on some shore with their money — I don't suppose they'd want the ship, fearful old white elephant . . . meanwhile, passengers dead, whatever else.' 'Would life go on as normal?' 'It would depend on their demands. A discreetly-managed hi-jacking would simply mean a few empty places at dinner and some strange faces on the bridge and in the radio-cabin, the visit of a helicopter, and the taking-off of some unidentified people, a tenseness in the staff and a sudden relaxation . . .' 'It could be going on at this moment in that case . . .' But my last remark displeased the Second Officer and he swung away to talk to another guest. I eyed the stout man at my elbow with a doubtful smile, wondering whether to introduce myself. He bent confidingly towards me. 'Have you heard about our murder?' he asked.

* * *

The tall, grim-mouthed stewardess swung the trolley-basket round the corner with an impatient jerk of her elbows. She strode pushing the cumbersome vehicle at a dangerous rate along the quiet corridor. A passenger, aglow in black-and-white tuxedo, stepped out of his cabin door and the stewardess wheeled her trolley sharply to avoid him. Some snowy towels fell out on to the floor striking the ground with a thump, as though heavy materials were wrapped in these towels. The stewardess bent quickly to pick them up, turning her back on the passenger who paused for a moment doubtfully. He had cut himself shaving and was a little drunk. 'Whaa you got in those towels eh? Ssshem . . . Sssstem . . . Sten guns?' The woman glared at him, and then with a sudden gesture shook out the towels which were empty of anything but their snowy whiteness. She shook them again thoughtfully, then bundled them up into a dirty-linen compartment of the trolley. 'You do not realize how well we take care of you, Sir,' she said with a charming smile that made her look like a beautiful woman.

* * *

Love and murder on the boat. What more could one hope for? This great vehicle in which people arrange themselves by class and cabin, suite and cubbyhole, from dance-band to dance-band, from favourite chair to ping-pong table, this place of soft carpeting and salty deck-boards, of deck tennis and sudden sunburn, ought to contain caverns and monsters. A death at sea, how clean. With a silver knife, done on clean sheets. A pang after loving: the soul goes voyaging on, the body is a clean husk in the refrigerator. All the English lessons, the schoolmarm clothes, the deodorants, simply walked out of, naked, through that neat hole of birth. It is not lonely, but clean, to die at sea, like the little mermaid, to blow away in spume. Why, that steward, the chief one, with his security officers on the one hand, and his waiters on the other, he is as a good sailor should be, able to turn his hand and his organization to anything. His spectrum merges into police force on the one side, and to nanny in the children's room on the other; he descends and becomes the gymnast in the yoga-class, he ascends smoothly in the lifts and brings the captain his off-duty glass of rum; in the Bank he cashes the cheques of travellers, or in the office he docks the pay of defaulters. His skin is clean and dry, his uniform is laundered, and he is the one who ferries us over the Atlantic, or if we wish to go further, he will keep our corpse unrotted to be claimed by such landlubbers who still remain (being unacquainted with the Atlantic spray and salt sunshine) interested in such things as the discarded parts of a developed adventurer. And even if she did not desire death at the hand of her lover, the hand that released her into love could not show her much love in this world and might (for all we know) be showing her exceeding love in the next. The neat stewards preside, and the service will be read over the man or woman who wishes to join the sea, whose step over the stern rails into the propeller-wake, the great biting conch, will be read not over the small cocoon-body wrapped in a laundered sheet, but over the whole sea, sheeting, unsheeting.

* * *

This ship in which a hi-jack or a murder is smoothly arranged into the working of the great black-and-white hierarchy, is nevertheless not a machine. It is a ship of blood. Blood waits on the tables, with plates of bloody meat. Earth-blood of fuel drives the engines. Blood stands behind the counters of the shopping arcade, selling diamonds and cameras. I hand the blood a five pound note, blood nods politely, it is a tip, blood-money. Money is the life blood of this society. Blood hands blood to the blood.

Animals are driven into the holds to be eaten. Some great engine distils pure water for the baths and drinking water. The fruits that cannot walk are basket cases to be carried until they are eaten. The Captain's lips dance in his linen face. We travel in the branching corridors like blood-fruit, 1500 of us, like a bee-comb, black and white bees attending black and white combs full of honey of blood.

The white uniforms flutter around table, full of blood. Cocktails: Bloody Mary, in much demand. English Rose, it is her period. Port-and-starboard, red light, green light. Cuba Libre, after much bloodshed. Trailing behind us, a white bloodless churning wake, into which the seabirds dip.

Like the sloughed skin of a snake stretching 2500 miles from shore to shore.

Like a comet's tail.

My blood beats in my neck, it is necessary to me, it is tourist-class blood, I cannot slough it off, I cannot ride the comet.

To be in America I must travel there in my body.

The horizon ruled straight as a hair cutting an egg.

* * *

When I was a small boy I had an assortment of boats and animals to take floating in my bath with me. I liked the battered and sucked boats that nobody would think of rigging with sails for any public exhibition on the pond in the park, I liked the boats that were junk. I liked the headless Mickey Mouse made of rubber, I believed that any shadowed water poured from his body was deadly poison. I would have preferred fragments of timber and torn rubber balls, but my mother became fastidious about my health and what was allowed to remain on the bathroom shelf. I would have preferred seaweed.

But these tossed and beaten articles of rubbish had the magic power of converting the bath to an ocean and my body to the lands of mystery and the krakens that unwary sailors would land upon, only to be flooded to their doom by my abrupt withdrawal of a knee, or the sucking in of my abdomen, or the expulsion of my breath. My hands were the winds that drove their boats and the gods that invisibly to them intervened. Sometimes my hands were these adventurers: Dr Fu Manchu would stand on his poop-deck wrapped in the gorgeous robe of a face flannel wrung as dry as possible, and plunge to his doom, getting his best clothes disgracefully wet, time and time again, as Nayland Smith overcame him — until the next episode. Half-hours would pass in this play until the earth-god's skin was all white and wrinkled with the soapy water, the sea topped up again and again from the hot tap.

Now this ocean on which I am travelling for the first time diminishes me. I stand like a sacrifice on the deck in my best clothes. I am an imaginary creature imagined in the hand that supports me. Some unsuspected ability has given me entirely into the care of this being, whose visible appearance is black and white, but whose real nature is blood. Would I now go unprotesting to my death as Fu Manchu did, or with some theatrical dwindling scream? As for the girl killed on the boat, did she go calmly because of the boat's calm, and did her murderer accept the inevitability of capture, and its black-white formalities, without protest? How was he discerned among the other passengers; he could surely have hidden even beyond the ending of the voyage, did the boat force a confession by its unruffled example? That girl was my lover too, if I had been accused, would I have gone quietly as they asked? The murderer must for a moment have believed himself to be powerful, but then a squall showed him in an instant what a murderer the ocean is, and what a saviour the boat.

* * *

However early I get up, and stand in the living-room (where the drapes are drawn overnight to provide ventilation for good slumber) to perform my pranayam, the great cars are still gliding smoothly by. The campus is green, and the trees of it throb and pulse in the wind, and the yellowing leaves that scrape at the screen windows enter my meditation, but along the roads that curve like lemniscates through the emerald fields, the great cars glide; threads through silk from earliest light. They are as quiet as punts on the river or liners on the ocean, their design is utterly at variance with the trees they pass under or the actions of the wind their lines are presumed to stream: their designs resemble blunt mineral snapped from the rocks, gleaming at the fractures, conchoidal, with streaks of silver and fool's gold. The windscreens glide the reflective landscape and from where I sit cross-legged, doing my deep-breathing, it is not easy to be sure that the cars contain people. Where are these people travelling? There must be all-night sittings of the University Senate, or early administration meetings, or lectures on the rising of the sun and the setting of the moon, with field work and telescope sightings. The tiny observatory sits in the long grass of an upper meadow quite still and natural to the scene; perhaps this is because when it glides, it glides on its own axis, as a tree does, but if it plucked its dome from the turf, then it would glide as these cars do, and resemble them. They are travelling mechanisms for watching behind glass, and this uneasy observation never ceases, this uneasy travelling in the smoothest machines in the world. I have ridden in them, the seats are like dentists' or abortionists' chairs, the landscape goes past like a picture projected on glass by the smoothly-running engine whose only indication that a mile is passing in a minute is the speedometer, and the people outside are figures in some drama on television.

* * *

In my day knowledge of four languages, one of them *not* an Indo-European tongue, was considered absolutely necessary for a young doctorate. The committees before which one's dissertation was defended often questioned one in any of the elected tongues, or cited some reference further afield. I fear that has all gone nowadays. The degree is handed out with a pleasant smile, for a pleasant smile, particularly to the good-looking. The combination of the young good looks and the high degree is to some I know an irresistible combination, like a nude reclining on an antique sofa, or a whore playing a Stradivarius. *(Which to the whore Professor, the candidate or the violin?)* I meant that these languages are the most exquisite instrument on which the developed sensitivity may play a considered view of the world, to its small audience of considered sensitivities. the dissertation is filed until needed, and the young man or woman walks out properly rubber-stamped and qualified to lecture to others like him or her but some six or seven years younger. That is as it is today; in my time you could reasonably wager on a reading knowledge of three European languages and one non-Indo-European tongue. *(What about a knowledge of post-Einstein physics and post-Freud psychology?)* The professor jumped. The Visitor, warm from his lecture, was clutching a paper cup of black coffee, his eyes showing their white. Old-fashioned, my dear Sir. (*I agree, shouted the Visitor. With Einstein being old-fashioned. You're not old-fashioned.*) Nor did I take it so, said the old Professor, the whites showing round his eyes.

* * *

All I can remember from that evening was the clitoris expert, and the sight of a great diamond blazing. I had been invited to lecture in this remote university almost on the Canadian border. My friend Alexander had offered to drive me there, it would be a holiday, he said, from his wife. We arrived, and were immediately taken out again for drinks. Then we made a round of the three sorority houses, and I talked about poetry to three separate and distinct masses of young women. The most pleasant aspect of this was that they moved in rhythm as they sat, like a field of corn in the wind, or like a willowy grove (for most of them wore their hair long) in a dawn wind. At the end of this ordeal I motioned to my sponsor that I wished to finish. He came forward to bring the meeting to a close. I had the sensation of being some rich man having read his own will aloud from his wheelchair, now wheeled away by his attorney to die properly, but maybe to linger on. 'A man of fortune greeting heirs.' Then it was time for dinner in an off-campus restaurant lit by red-shaded bulbs. I was quite drunk by this time, and as I sat down at table I realized that if I drank much more I would be unable to stand. Yet I had my main lecture to deliver! Despite the solicitations of my friends, I drank little and ate as much as possible. However, it was too late for sobriety, and it was at this point that I began to lose the evening. I delivered my lecture, but my difficulty in thinking and speaking was providentially masked by the strong echo in the college chapel. Any speaker there would be obliged to adopt a halting delivery, drunk or sober. I remember the echo coming back, and how I would have to pause while my accumulated words fell back on me from ceiling and walls, how I would stare at the rivery grain of the lectern while this process completed itself, and bow I would lose all recollection of my theme in contemplation of the wooden river, and would start again by picking up some poem from my books. These were good poems, and I suppose cemented the collage by being full enough of energy to become relevant to any statement. I suppose that the students and staff were accustomed by the properties of their place of worship to these collages. Their minds would leap ahead in the assumption that their speaker knew what he was saying, and make sense of his discourse that way. What excellent creative training, and no wonder they gave their visitors so many drinks. I know that I must have made sense, one way or another, since before I left they asked me to stay on as a member of faculty.

Now, having delivered myself of whatever my audience by goodwill and guesswork could make sense of, my exhaustion caused the rest of the evening to be entirely a fog, but for the two clear perceptions I have spoken of, the expert on the clitoris, and the great flashing diamond. The former I can now account for; the latter not at all. The clitoris expert was a specialist in Blake who was, if possible, drunker than I, myself. It was his house we ended up at. His walls were covered with many beautiful books, in particular a full set of facsimiles of Blake's prophetic books. With an impatient gesture, this man cleared the table of knives and forks and plates, shoving them with his forearm to one side, and spilling a glass of gin over the cleared patch. Into this patch he hefted off the shelves volume after volume of facsimile, with none too clean drunken fingers tugging at the pages, showing me design after design and shouting: 'Look! Clit! Clit! Mrs Blake's Clitoris, look here, in the margin, among those vines. The worm in the sick rose. The period! The bloody wife!' He was telling me that he saw this organ 'The opener, the closer, the hooded guardian at the gate' as the preoccupation of William's wife, who at her menstrual period preferred her own eroticism to Blake's, and who screamed at the great poet when she felt this time of her period coming upon her, 'The White Giant is breaking up!' He showed me textbook after textbook of gynaecology with the clitoris developed (as it will) to various sizes, almost to the size of a male penis in hermaphrodites. He showed me places in Blake's text where the poet inveighed against the hermaphrodite in mankind, and where he praised the holy marriage. I remember these pictures passed in front of my eyes, though I was too drunk to comment. I nodded in the right way, for the Professor clapped me on the back many times, and urged me to stay in the town. But as for the diamond! I remember a black box opened and this great diamond sitting on black velvet with that sparkle that cannot be counterfeited, and I remember the black box closing, and my drunken tears at the beauty of the gem. But who in this small university town would own a diamond the size of a small plum?

I think it was this Professor who played me Verdi's 'Requiem' which I had not heard before. In the morning, that music was still with me, though I could not tell whether I had listened to a gramophone record, or buried my face and hands in many different brocades, whose figured texture still ran over my skin like music.

* * *

The best benders I remember were those when I woke up in the wrong bed. Once I lost the worst hangover of my life when a lady hairdresser cut my hair in the kitchen the morning after. If a woman I had not known previously took me to bed after I had been drinking, I would awake with no hangover, but rather, full of love. If I collapsed while drinking and they helped me to bed

— as often happened — I used to call this my 'dream of soft hands and kind voices.' At that time I drank instead of sleeping around, and, fuckwise, I was still faithful to my wife. I used instead to put myself in the way of these tremendous alcoholic cuddles, these beautiful free dreams of soft hands and long hair. I cannot remember trying to fuck these women, but that cannot have offended them, for I continued to find my way to their beds.

It was shortly before my marriage broke up that I began to sleep around. This was not the cause of the breakup, but the effect. I hoped to acquire sexual authority that would bring my wife closer to me, but I could not gain that authority solely with the one woman I had begun my fucking-life with. I do not believe that during those fraught eighteen months I ever had an experience as satisfactory as those dreams of soft hands and velvet voices. Not until I began to sleep with you; and then, except at times of trial, I no longer want to drink.

* * *

The hatches battened over blood. A white blood-fly with black wing-cases sailing over the water-skin. A white and black blood-stallion snorting smoke-plumes. In the night, chains rattle in the holds. The Captain clothes and reclothes his blood in white duck. He raises his hand to his right eyebrow in a polite salute. The eye is bloodshot from cigarette smoke, from hangovers caught in his solitary bed. What steers the ship? The young officers steer the ship, cut the meat, swab the wounds, lay the tables, send the radio messages. The Captain winks, his orderly presses a glass of rum on the Professor (who does not drink), the Captain conceals a belch behind his hand, it is a blood-bubble.

We sail beneath a blood-bubble, Sirius winks fierily, the bubble is pricked by the fiery sparks, a fine blood-rain falls drenching the white duck, a new sky bubble composed of the black blood of the dead reforms. The Captain changes his bloody uniform. A ball carries the mate's arm away, 'You blasted buggers,' he howls. 'I'm maimed,' he howls, 'for seven quid a day.' The sound-box of his guitar fills slowly with blood. The quoits he plays on the deck stick to the deck because of blood. The burgundy is blood.

I rattle the dice in the cup and throw them, a gout of fresh blood splashes the clean tablecloth. 'Steward,' I yell, 'change this dirty tablecloth.' The clanking of chains in the hold is the churning of the automatic laundry. The long chain of stewardesses with stained and bloody laundry diminishes as more machines are pressed into service. Blood and water pour from the vents at the side of the vessel. The sun rises like raw meat. With our sails broken we are driven away on the dawn wind. Our bottom is raked off by the coral reef. We sink, and our wounds are washed clean, our bodies made bloodless, and our bones fleshless by the sea and its prickle-toothed children.

Give me a Bloody Mary, howls the Captain to his scurrying orderly, who smirks at the violence he himself has inflamed in his master by a constant urging of drinks on him from his silver tray, always full, always rocking the bell-like ice-cubes, always censing the gentle alcoholic perfumes among the guests.

* * *

I discovered on my return that the Principal had built a large barn-like auditorium at the back of the college. The walls as I inspected them were as yet undressed breeze-block, and the place had the air of an immense military bunker abandoned by the Germans. I asked to look at the plans. In effect it was to be a very fine small theatre; the trouble was that even the smallest theatre — above the size of the one of our ordinary lecture-rooms that is — was bound to be too big for our number of students. I asked whether programmes had been devised for the building. It appeared that touring theatrical companies were to be invited, and that one new full-time member of the staff was to be appointed to take charge of the theatre and to run classes in dramatics and associated skills. I could see that the whole thing was a ploy to make the college more 'visible' in the world: the Quality would visit, and the players would play, and travel on, and a few students would spend a week or two learning to mouth and gesticulate, sit glumly, pretend to be trees or firing-squads, then they would give up and go back to their painting. Meanwhile there would be another member of staff sitting tight, teaching nothing, growing greyer and greyer from self-disgust and non-productivity. He would pass through the usual phases of enthusiasm, laying himself out completely for entirely imaginary students, giving all this time to these mythical creatures, then he would begin affairs with real students in a glow of idealism turning to fucking, persuading himself there was no other way to impregnate them with his being; then he would buy a large house and settle down to drawing his permanent staff salary without a care in the world except that of knowing he was an empty, idiotic, useless husk. In due time he would grow by duration and persistence to some rank in the college, and then he would spend his time on committees interfering out of his deadness of spirit with any creativity that did manage a brief flowering in this wilderness of old artists and phoney artists.

I thought I would please the librarian. 'Colleges grow great if their libraries grow,' I said, 'better by far to have made more lecture-rooms or library-space.' 'They want encounter groups and psycho-drama in my library,' he said gloomily, 'I'd rather they had them in there.' I watched the green trees nod at the long windows and remembered my first excitement at having been appointed to a college of the arts.

* * *

The new theatre glowed with its light African pine panelling. An anonymous donation had completed it, and added a green room, fine small dressing-rooms, and a theatre library with a tiny bar and clubroom. A fund had been established to invite solo artists as well as touring companies. The seats rose in deep semi-circular tiers, and the hall was not crowded, though every seat was occupied.

The black singer was watery with diamonds. She sang an arrangement of Elgar's *Sea-Pictures* for unaccompanied voice. She was known for the enormous range of her voice; in this piece it seemed that there were two singers, one the chief contemplator of the sea, the other the sea itself. I had noticed before the concert began that most of our students were in the theatre. This was an unusual attendance, normally a proportion of them preferred to boycott an event for the sake of the gesture, and one seldom saw them *en masse* except for films. This was the first time I had seen a good attendance at a concert. Local people made up the rest of the audience. This again was an unusual thing, as the locals preferred to shun the college, particularly in early summer, when the tourist trade was beginning.

This black lady held our little college spellbound. Our brochure emphasized its situation by the sea, but I believe that none of us had seen the sea at all until that black lady began to sing about it to our memories. Nothing before her song had brought all the tiny pieces of observation, the full moon making a great stepladder across the water one midnight; the bright shaking rock-pools in midsummer; the white birds grown dirty and draggled with winter-pecking at an oily sea deserted by visitors; the great grey anvils of cloud that rose out of our sea like scaffoldings for immense archaic temples; walks on the sand fiddling with seaweed, popping the bladders, somebody's driftwood bonfire in the next bay; pockets full of pebbles and mantelpieces lined with them; the dreary slow shuffling of the cold visitors through the town on dull days; the flashing smiles and loud alien voices on sunny days — we all had pictures like this in our minds but never before the black lady came to sing to us had we fitted them together so that they became one feeling, one existence. She stood there and sang and held us enchanted and made us companions in perception; she had seen, and she made us see. The tides moved through us, we travelled the moonlit stepladder and the moon was a syllable in a sentence that was being sung by a lady black as the night in which the moon rode, the bright dazzling rock-pools were notes she had heard and could repeat, the deserted beaches were an aching pause in the music without which the music would not have moved in its surges, the anvils of cloud rang like throats across the sea, the salt seaweed wove ideas in the shallow waves, the sea-fire leapt up with faster rhythm, the pebbles clocked in the surge with a deeper sound, the visitors were glad to join us and we gave them the sentences of our life together in the good place of sea-rhythms. The singing finished, the sea-college held its breath for an instant, for all breathing had been done by proxy, by the black singer, and then it made the sea-noise of applause.

* * *

He sliced off the top of his thumb on one of the planing-machines. A great shout! And blood all over the wood-shavings, like an arena of sawdust — I closed my eyes and smelt the sun and cried Olé! — I opened my eyes and there was my friend hopping about trying to get his hankie out of the pocket on the side of the wound with his uninjured hand, smearing himself with blood across the front of his trousers, across the seat, popping the juicing thumb into his mouth and gagging because too much was flowing, his teeth bloodstained like Dracula, pulling up the tail of the shirt to staunch his thumb. 'Joseph, here', said the assistant and offered him the sliced thumb-cap in his outstretched palm. With bright interest we tried to fit the little piece of meat and nail to the slickly flowing satin decap, the wrong way round to begin with so that the nail opposed the palm, then correctly, binding it up in ripped striped work-shirt. My friend looked white as the face of one of his racing dogs, and like them, his eyes were pale and the colour of unripe mushroom gills, a bleached slate. We made him sit down while the assistant fetched his car to take him up the hill to the accident ward of the hospital.

'How's your thumb, Joe?' He held out a great bandaged dolly. One of the graduate students took out his felt-tip and drew a headless nude on the white gauze. 'That's not right,' Joe said. 'The chopped-off piece grew in.' A fortnight later nothing could be seen on the nail; it had grown upward, displacing the broken part. The splice was visible in the flesh of the thumb, a thin red line, slightly puckered with scar-tissue, like a hangman's noose biting deeply. The blow of the blade had made the thumb slightly stiff at the joint, but a month after the accident my friend was at his trade of wood-butcher once again. He remarked to me that the sea-air had a healing Jesus-touch, as when the ear of the high priest's servant had grown back into the hurt head at Jesus's hands. He said that he wouldn't mind going through the experience again, for the beautiful feeling of being restored, for the sense of healing.

* * *

In my mind The Glass Cottage is that tiny and compact house with the thatch by the stream in Boscastle village. One turns off the high street and passes several gardens all plump with shiny leaves and loamy flowerbeds, with the green path very soft under the feet, and the cart-track swings round to the right and downhill to the little valley of oak trees through which that shallow active stream runs. Perched on its bank is The Glass Cottage. It is of light stone that will take a glow from the sunshine and a pale radiance from the darkness — it is a local quartz stone — and its windows are plain ordinary glass, except that this glass seems to have more to reflect since it is by the water, that busily breaks up the light like a quivering limb of electricity lying among enormous dock leaves big as tables and moss quiet as a yogin at prayer. Indeed I had imagined the softness and green vibrancy of this moss made up of the lotus postures of millions of transcending fat bodhisattvas so great that they had become numerous and small, and dedicated to softening footsteps in the resilience and pliability of their entranced bodies. If I looked closely I could see the crown of petals springing from the head of each master contemplative, a man well on his way to disappearing into the atom. I believe my thoughts may have taken this direction as there is a teashop in the village on the way called 'The Green Buddha'.

I have visited this cart-track, and felt my feet pacing it of themselves until the path opened up to reveal The Glass Cottage, perhaps a score of times. The quality of the Cottage is that on these occasions it remains empty. The owner never reveals himself, perhaps because the Cottage is waiting for me, its true owner. But as yet I have not got the key. I know that the Cottage is occupied, I have noticed bottles and glasses appear and disappear from a table spread with a brown cloth in the right-hand window, and there is not always a little car in the garage to the left, but I have no evidence that I do not live there in another state of mind, or in another time. I never peer closely into the windows in case I catch myself washing up, or pouring a glass of Guinness or masturbating, or doing push-ups; or in case I catch another person doing these things and I am compelled to arrest him as a burglar. I have many photographs of the Cottage, snapped surreptitiously from the cart-track, or from further up the path where there is a kissing-stile; I would not care for the owner, myself, to catch me taking photographs of my own cottage out of which I stalk brandishing my stick and slamming the front door, angry at the liberty. I believe that the figure would not come out on the film if I held the camera, and would appear among all that colour of green and bright water, light stone and glass reflecting the busyness of the stream, the cream painted wooden front door and the beehives in the front garden, as a white silhouette, sheer blank white. Often there is a red tinge over the photographs taken in the evening which I cannot account for.

Further up the path, walking upstream, there is a perfect holy valley of oaks and beeches and a meadow that swells to a round mump. In this valley is a tree standing by itself whose boughs are so tightly pleached that it looks like a great circular basket on a stalk. To sit in this valley and do one's pranayama is to see visions of battles, cavalry and swift masculine death, and visions of the peace secured and watched over by these deaths. The Glass Cottage is a fitting hermitage by the singing water at the gate of this valley. At the time of the last visit, the water of the Atlantic was already lapping at my feet and at the foundation of my life, and the great liner had placed my name on its black and white rosters ready to float me off across the ocean chasm between the two worlds.

* * *

The first time in my adult life I tried to do push-ups I could manage three. It was my boast that I had done no exercise since leaving school; yet the air of England had become aggressive and I felt I needed to learn how to defend myself. I needed to become stronger. Accordingly, I began strengthening exercises, including push-ups.

After daily practice, at the end of eighteen months I was able to push thirty times with ease, another five with less ease, and a total of forty, if I persisted. I had become stronger; my shoulders had filled out, and I wanted to learn to use my new strength. I joined a judo club, but took such a fall at the beginner's weekend that I feared that my ribs were cracked. Nevertheless, in a couple of months' time I rejoined, this time more seriously, and with the determination to lose weight so that my falls would not be so injuriously heavy. I was scared of these falls, which made my judo over-defensive, but I progressed through the coloured grades, from the white belt with red tips that denoted the utter beginner, in a skip to orange at the one grading, from orange to green and from green to blue. I was very proud of the bright and dangerous belt around my hips, vivid against my white judo clothes — dangerous that is to novices: to have a blue belt grading is to be, as the Japanese say, only the second grade of beginner.

At this time I was in good training, and most of my judo practice was with men ten years or so my junior — I was thirty-five. I continued with my push-ups, but had reached my limit with these exercises: forty pushes. I could, however, do several groups of these in short succession. But how I met an unexplained phenomenon. I wanted to increase the number of pushes, because rightly or wrongly, I believe that these were an index of my strength and stamina. But I could not go above forty — except at night, if I performed them in a darkened room. Then it was fifty, and once a delirious sixty. A darkened room . . .

She never seemed to notice the hardness of my developed body. The other woman seduced me by running her hands over my arms and shoulders and praising my big muscles.

* * *

The man with the big nose and drawn-down mouth sat at the piano on the stage of the cinema hall. He was practising, the lights were turned up. He played a Chopin Mazurka, some Gershwin, then much that was unidentifiable since it was a practice melding of composers, a great plunge from Beethoven to Janáček. Then he filled the hall with simple waves of sound, gentle music imitating the liner itself, ablaze with lights on the ocean like a great glass cottage, a glass castle, a glass mountain, a black and white iceberg with a soft piano at its heart. As the piano played in silence, the iceberg melted and released music that was the waves of the sea rising and covering the ship. It sunk unprotesting into the waves. All the passengers were spellbound, mouths open, asprawl in their cinema seats as the water gently rose about them and the contents of their lungs wove out through the water like silvery exploding fish. Seaweed fastened to the piano undulating in waves, the polished black surface became speckled with barnacles. The music stopped, started again. The lights dimmed. The pianist rose, the dim stage-lights glinting in his bald head, and walked with a measured pace to the footlights. With slow grace he bent towards me and caught my eye. 'Wouddja tell me what time it is?' he said in Brooklynese. 'Time for the film.' 'Poifect.' Slowly he paced across the stage towards the wings on the opposite side to the piano. A scattering of applause rose for his playing. Then The Valachi Papers began to project themselves over his disappearing back. He turned, and bowed his thanks, and in the darkness a gangster bled down his big nose and white shirt.

* * *

My friend Max had found a new way of combining portraiture and poetry. Already an accomplished poet, he had now begun to employ models to dress up and paint their faces according to his wish. There would be much brooding and walking up and down then he would suddenly fling himself down at big typewriter and start typing furiously. The work was always a poem about the model, but arranged in such a way on the page that it was also a portrait of her face or of the attitude of her figure. He told me that he had become so accustomed to the typewriter during all his years as a freelance writer that this facility was simply a natural development. In fact, it redeemed those wasted years not only in that it was an artistic discovery arising out of them, but also in that his typewritten portraits caught on and sold well — being treated as works of visual art rather than poems and therefore reproduced in the glossy art magazines in full colour for enormous fees and not for the pittances that poetry commands. He ordered a typewriter with a specially small typeface in which no letter was larger than a pinhead, and his skill became more manifest — he could reproduce by the arrangement of his poem the effect exactly of a newspaper photograph that was grainy and yet clear. All the effects of depth and perspective, tone and shading, were possible and even easy to him, and the picture possessed the added dimension of poetical meaning, a further level of exploration. There was controversy as to whether the poetic meaning or the pictorial was initial or paramount, and many critics made certain fees by drawing lengthy comparisons. I asked him what he thought. 'Well,' he said, adjusting a new contrivance on his typewriter, a four-coloured broad ribbon that would give him a full-colour effect, 'during all those years of writing reviews and articles, and never quite catching up with the work or the bills, and people never paying up on time, I used to have streaks of good luck that at first I couldn't account for. Then I grew superstitious, as I thought, and made little bets with myself, that if for instance I chose a margin to my MS that was exactly an inch broad, my work would be accepted, if it was seven-eighths of an inch broad, it would be returned, and if it was an inch and one eighth, I would be offered a fee higher than usual. I kept a notebook and a chart, and made a detailed record of my predictions. It varied the monotony of freelance work, and I think that work actually improved, since I was looking at it only with the corner of my eye, and not full-face, as it were, and so, like a star, I was able to see it more clearly.

'I had stepped out of and back from my rut. But I remember the day of the real breakthrough. It was a dull day, and there was a thunderstorm outside impending but not yet breaking. I had the wireless on and every now and again a burst of static broke across the music showing that the thundercloud had already started broadcasting lightning, but not on the visible spectrum. I went across to the switches to turn on the light, reminding myself that the bill was not paid, and that I would be using electric light to write my piece that would pay for the electric light by which I wrote it. Suddenly there was a god-awful crash of thunder and the fuses blew. The room was almost pitch dark. I swore and threw the typescript in my hand across the room. I could see the pages rasping and fluttering through the heavy air like stormy petrels. Then there was a flash of bright lightning and in the flash I saw my room lit as with photo-floods — but it was not empty! I had an unexpected visitor. A naked woman was stretched on my sofa. Her head was raised and her eyes were

storms and dripping water-fruit on to its broad leaves of ocean and the broad soil, which it delves and sustains. Why when we hear the climax of Liszt's *Faust Symphony* or the Berlioz opera, these moments of climax and damnation, of sadness and power, do we hear rejoicing and ability? When Faust goes down, the voices contradict by rigour and vehemence their story of decline. Why, the words of Verdi's requiem ask apology but throb with libidinous blood, it is a church of blood! I saw and was present at a service in the church of blood on three occasions. The first was a school production of the Bacchae; Dionysus entered, golden haired and white-horned, his robes and fingers dripping with blood; the blood in us shivered as the power of god passed through its branches. Then there was the communion service in Exeter Cathedral, so brightly lighted that all (in their dusty broadcloth) looked shabby (in their decent suits) and the priest in his magnificent canonicals was an apparition of flame at the altar of flame who graciously allowed them to confess their sins and kneel when he served them with his chalice of blood squeezed from grapes grown in soil of blood; that priest walked behind a thick stone pillar and I felt the beam of power cut off from me by that pillar of the church. And the third epiphany was called the play *Sleuth* and there was this ridiculous inspector groping for clues on the spiral staircase where a murder was pretended and no murder was. 'Blood, Sir,' said the Inspector. 'Blood?' said the novelist, the man of paper blood, of black veins of print. 'Blood,' replied the inspector, and touched a patch of shadow on the stair that seemed tacky. 'In that case, Sir, what is Blood doing on your staircase?' I felt and saw the pale petalled flower of the audience's faces opening like a great cunt down their breathless throats to where they joined together. 'Blood, inspector? How can there be blood there?' 'Macbeth has never moved me,' mused the Ship's Doctor, 'it is too polite in production, I like the blood smeared with an erotic feeling, like a mixture of paint and clay. When I saw my first real brain, grey slippery cauliflower, I vomited into the trepan. Later I became callous, and ate my ham sandwiches during the neck dissection. There was a lecturer once at University Hospital who was an expert at that very difficult demonstration, the human neck dissection. His preparations were sought internationally by medical schools. One morning he awoke depressed, he had been depressed in the mornings for a month or two, and began to shave. He felt a lethargy grow as he brushed on the copious white foam. He splashed cold water onto his face and saw the cleared skin glow with love of fresh water. He opened his case of scalpels and forceps and deliberately gave his chin a nick. He was so good at dissection that he had never cut himself while shaving. The nick stimulated him with its little pain, but it did not please him. It demonstrated nothing, not without microscope. He swabbed his throat with alcohol. He injected novocaine. He dissected his neck open in the bathroom mirror. Then with pleasure he nicked the jugular and spoiled his dissection. Then he nicked the recurrent laryngeal nerve so that he could not cry out when his death approached and he grew weaker like a child. He was discovered, still standing upright in front of the bathroom mirror, a smile on his cold face and his throat an impenetrable mass of blood and his bare feet stuck to the floor with blood.' 'I am a doctor,' said the doctor, 'and I have met a lot of loonies in my time, but never one who met death standing.' 'His ghost, bubbling horribly, is said to haunt the white-black corridors of the hospital with its torn rag of technicolour,' said the doctor, quaffing a little cup of peppermint and magnesia and replacing the waxy sheet over the face of the beautiful dead woman who had come to him with a lover's face and a slit in her liver one hour before. His watch ticked loudly. He looked at it and saw that it had stopped. A watch ticked loudly. The sound was coming from the dead woman's trolley. He lifted the sheet again and inspected her wrists. They were naked. He put his ear to her lips, then to her silent chest — here the ticking was loud. He passed his ear down her body; *the* ticking came from her wound. With practised fingers he felt inside the stiff lips of the wound, inside he found something stonier than the small gravelly blood-clots. He eased it out into the light. She was beginning to smell slightly, like a dried tooth. The object he had found in her wound was a small gold bracelet watch, of the kind that is worn in the evening, with a good long dress, at a ship's dance, among the white uniforms and black ties, when the passengers contrast with the formally-clad ship's personnel and resemble gaily-coloured waste cast out on the strict and dangerous ship's wake coiling white into the night sea.

* * *

The Professor watched the dance from one of his favourite seats, at a small table in an alcove where there was a porthole. In this manner he could watch both inside and outside with a turn of his bearded head. Tonight he noticed a curious detail about the ship's personnel, in contrast with the passengers. Of course the officers and stewardesses were dressed in severe black and white, with a touch of gold braid on the shoulders to denote their rank, and the glint of two brass buttons at the abdomen, and though this emphasized the gaudy evening dress of the passengers — even the men no longer kept to a black jacket for the evening, where they were formally dressed it was in tartan or lamé — this was not the most striking difference between the two kinds of people. As the couples dancing neared and passed his table, the Professor began counting to be sure. He entered the results in his customary small notebook that he used for all observations. Yes, that was quite certain. The men dressed in white and black blinked very much less often than the people dressed in coloured clothes. The latter blinked on an average of once every two or three seconds; the ship's people on the other hand blinked perhaps once every five or six seconds — one man he thought was the ship's doctor was wide-eyed for no less than ten seconds, by the little hand on the Professor's gold wristwatch. He could not imagine why this should be so, and determined to watch again for the phenomenon at various times of the day in varying circumstances. Perhaps, he thought, it was some ability to watch sustainedly distant horizons on the part of the sea-faring folk, as he timed his own eyelids. I must be falling asleep, he called drowsily to himself as the white face of his watch's dial slid off his wrist bending and splashing like a plate of water in his face — 'Ah!' and he sat up with a jerk, 'Jactitation! Again.' As he rose to go to his cabin he felt disinclined to repeat his observations about the eyelids of the ship's personnel, and the thought of a paragraph in 'Notes and Queries' no longer gave him any pleasure, since poor Professor, he was getting old, bags of slack skin had begun to form under his eyes, and though this looked good on television, it was still a feeble kind of joke to say that one should run ahead of the sun, as this boat was now doing, and gain time.

* * *

The fat man paused, fascinated by the white patterns on the promenade deck. 'Look at this,' he said to his companion, a thin, small, elderly man dressed in a white suit and wearing a white straw hat with a black band, 'it's like hopscotch.' 'I think it's deck quoits,' said the older man. His face and neck were immensely freckled with old people's freckles, the irregular staining of the skin like maps drawn on vellum; his eye-whites even were freckled with yellow. 'You fling these heavy stones in a certain manner and they come to rest in the numbered spaces.' 'They'd slide into the sea.' 'No, that's not how you throw them.' 'I'm disappointed. I thought it was hopscotch.' 'You're too fat to dance hopscotch.' 'I couldn't bend for deck quoits. Jeremy, lend me ten pounds.' As he said this last, the fat man wrinkled his face up as though he was going to cry. Without looking at him, his dapper companion dipped in his hip pocket and took out a black leather wallet, extracted a browny-green ten-pound note, folded it carefully lengthwise and passed it to his friend like a spill. Their stride hastened down the long deck until with a sharp turn to the right they went through a steel door. The old man put his hand to the crown of his hat as they passed the dining-room ventilator blowing out to sea its distillate of food smells and scent smells and soap smells and sweat smells, but he breathed this person-brandy with pleasure. The Professor, on the other hand, always held his breath as be passed the ventilator. Today the latter was sleeping late, and missed his usual walk in the air before breakfast. The deck became clear for a moment, then it was suddenly full of running children.

* * *

Blue hands, the colour of frozen water. Winter sky, very blue, with a few rinses or rags of dilute tissue-of-blood. Under the cut-out heatless sun, the dwarfed liner plies.

* * *

The university in the forest, in the lightly-forested meadows of the Catskills foothills. The great library in the forest, shining at night like a liner. The great library shining through its windows at the end of the willow-walk. The great library stuffed with light. Served with books by gentle stout homosexuals in vivid clothes walking like long-legged birds. Golden-trousered librarians, with paunches and pouts and very gentle voices dressed in light tan clothes and white clothes. The dustless, polished library in the forest with the avenue of willows that is like walking between the crests of two tall waves. The ruby ear-rings shining within the midnight afro hair.

* * *

The lake sits quiet among the trees like a brain of the university. The library sits above the lake like the cortex and memory of the university. The library dances quietly alight in the water of the lake like the satyr-brain of the university. Soon tradition (recorded in books of the library) will cause the students to dance round the lake with lighted torches, doubled in the quiet lake-water. The students with living torches will bloom in the lighted waters to become a part of the lake, the living fire blooming in the wood of the torches will be tinder to these students' memories. Water and fire and wood: the books in the lighted library tell of this scatteredly, there are sparks of this scene shown among the many, many pages, but it takes more than a library, it takes the reflective water shaking to unite the picture of goat-legs and white arms and to cause the dancing. It is not the books of recorded tradition that cause the dancing, but the presence of the reflective water to dance around. Within the water lie the living memories in alogical circuits of all the dances that have taken place there and the currents of the lake dancing combine and recombine them.

* * *

'Do you think that electron degeneracy is the clue to short-term memory in the brain?' I shouted along the bus. It was my stop, and I did not want to irritate the conductor by not being at the doors when he opened them. 'No,'shouted Endenberg along the aisle, bending forward so that I could see the fringe of white hair circling at the back of his pink skull, 'No, I consider short-term memory to be a function of hydrogen-bonding in the water of the brain.' 'Water on the brain, eh Professor,' I riposted as I swung out of the bus onto university avenue. 'What was that?' came faintly back to me through the open window as the bus accelerated away. But I had already forgotten the discussion as I stood amazed at the sun on the snow and the sun on the lake.

* * *

Water has very marvellous qualities. Any textbook will tell you that. It is a thing that students forget — they wash their hair in it, they drink it, they are made of it — two-thirds of them is water — it will need an obsessed professor, one obsessed by water as the water in his body brought from home is so swiftly replaced by water in the new place he lives in, and with it go all his sharp memories of home, of the immense mass of water that carries so many human memories and events across itself on that which resembles a part of it, the liner, but which is really a part of humankind, dressed in black and white, plying the great mass of undrinkable water, salt as blood. A glass of water is a crystal lattice for the molecule H_2o is a dipole -H o+ H- and the dipole forms a web of water-glitter that is a lattice like an immense snow-flake; a glass of water is a single molecule like a diamond crystal. The lattice is soft and deformable, it is altered in shape by a man passing, by the moon passing overhead. The Atlantic is just such a soft diamond that fits snugly into its shores, and is difficult to pass, except by something shaped like the liner snugging along its water-lines.

* * *

Inside the walls of the glass cottage, he finishes his prose poem about the American cicadas. He lifts his eyes from the table to the open window where the stream flashes, and is amazed to hear no sound of cicadas. His eyes go down again to his poem, and his ears are at once full again of the shrilling in the trees.

She comes in and puts a cup of tea on his table. 'I'm not disturbing . . . ?' 'No, I've finished. Would you like to go for a walk? In the silence.' 'Is anywhere silent? There is always the sound of the stream here. I couldn't do without the knowledge that I'm going to come home to that sound. Or that this sound can be found anywhere there is running water. 'Let's go to Forrabury.'

As they walked down the hill into the new part of the village, the air in the valley was essentially silent, even though it was overlaid with the noises of everyday living. Somebody was calling for his dog on the hill, the milkman was clanking his urns and his bottles in their wire racks. They turned to the left and climbed the hill towards Forrabury, the ancient church on the south headland. The breeze off the hill felt vibrant with its passage through the grasses and across the bare cliff faces. The preaching-cross on a mound by the lych-gate made them pause for a moment. Sometimes they preferred this granite shaft surmounted by the wheel-cross, to the church itself, that is, in high liturgical seasons. But now it was late summer, and the Christian year was long over. Now the older feelings of the church held sway from the ground beneath it.

The heavy wooden door of the church sealed them shut in its pillared gloom. The noise of it closing disturbed the echoes and they felt a moment's hostility towards them before the air currents settled. They were accustomed to this moment's alarm, as though the air in the church had been disturbed praying. Until it was over they stood still. For the air in the stone to examine them, and pass them, took about as long at their eyes becoming accustomed to the gloom. It accepted them, and they felt free once again to walk forward and find the place in the church they needed. He sat by the altar-steps, she on a pew near the front. Once the air had settled, they heard the shrilling again, a sound that seemed sometimes in their own ears, sometimes deep in the stone of the church, a humming as of wind through taut wires, shrill, but not faint once it was heard. It was always there, whether listened to or not. 'Our Father,' she prayed; 'Mother of God,' he prayed; 'Our Father, Brother, Lover,' she prayed; 'Our Mother, Sister, Lover,' he prayed; 'Eternal Child and God,' they prayed, 'Child of the Moon and Sun, restore us, errant people, to thy communion . . .' The singing in the stone accepted their prayer and steadied their minds, for it was the singing in their blood and in the hill's roots and in the sea. It was made of the sun's light, it was the sun's light made audible, and it was turned into a name by the circling of the moon. The whole world said this name as it circled the sun, as the sun circled its sun, and the name came as much from the red heart of the sun as from the red marrow of their bodies. The world inside accepted them, they stepped from the stone and the world outside accepted them.

* * *

They drove round the sharp curve and down the hill. Here the snow had begun to lie along the branches of the trees, on the pavement, and in the gutters of the road but not yet on the crown of it 'There's more snow coming,' said his Father, 'but I'll see you get to work if it's bad.' He knew his father would but there was always a strain between them on car journeys. He loved the bus, with its warm muggy smell and its wheezing doors. All those people crammed into it made it a country of faces and textures, the heavy wools of overcoats and mufflers, the cool leather of gloves, and the warm breath that had entered and left so many pairs of lungs comforted him, germ-laden though it might be. This great grunting bus-animal with its warm human freight always arrived, however bad the snow might be, sometimes a little late from climbing the snow-slippery hill, but it always came, whatever the weather, and it had run on time during the height of Hitler's war.

* * *

Many years ago the thin elderly man who thought it correct to wear white on an ocean-going vessel during the daylight hours had been a patient of the psychologist Jung. The former had been about fifty, and a successful journalist. He told the psychologist a dream which had made him dizzily happy. He had been standing on a mountain-peak on a cloudy day. Great sculptured clouds filled the sky and hid the sun. Suddenly a shaft of light broke from above and illuminated — no, tinged with gold — the opposite mountain peak, which was at least twenty miles away. A light rain began to fall, and with it the dreamer understood that he had above all, at any risk, to get to that peak opposite, that if he did so his life would be transformed into a most marvellous thing. At that the clouds began to clear off the sun, but it rained still and a magnificent rainbow appeared, first as a coloured patch hanging above the valley between the two mountains, then as a magnificent arch which sprang from his feet to the opposite peak. It was translucent, and so bright it seemed solid. He stepped forward and touched it — it was solid. With a sudden decision he ran out on to it and found that it gripped his feet so that he was able to run lightly to the crown of the bow, and there he found the texture changed and he could slide down astride it like a polished stair banister. Gripping the rainbow between his thighs he sped down towards the peak of his heart's desire — and woke up, laughing with joy, his pyjamas tacky with semen that had slipped out of him. The joy stayed with him for days, and he considered that the dream was the solution and culmination of his analysis.

Jung, however, was not so pleased. 'Human beings walk on the ground. On the earth. Only the gods walk rainbow bridges, and you are not a god. You are a man, and you must travel down the mountain and toil across the valley before you can ascend to the peak of your heart's desire.' Jung's grumpy words impressed his patient. He gave up his job at the newspaper, and went back to the university with a grant as a mature student, and using the savings which he would otherwise have spent on the analysis. In seven years he had his Ph.D. Now he had retired from university teaching. The death of an uncle had made him well-off. He enjoyed the companionship of men of middle-age who were beginning to realize that youth and opportunity were vanishing. He liked watching them put on weight, or adopt a sexually promiscuous life-style, or whatever means of self-discovery forced itself upon them. He would not intervene or advise, he would do no more than offer companionship and occasional assistance with small sums of money. He also maintained a small practice as a psychotherapist of young people.

Today he leaned over the rail of the black-white liner in his white clothes soaked in sunshine, watching the great slough-wake coiling its way back in the direction of England. He realized that he was travelling a bridge between two peaks of land on a black and white funicular held by water-cables over an immense watery abyss which would be, if he sank in it, little more resistant to a plunge than the rainbow valley of his dream. He would fall buoyed up like Alice or an insect down a mine, and he would be dead before he struck bottom and sent up his cloud-splash in the ooze. It was a black-white rainbow bridge but become more solid and matter-of-fact as befitted his age, and it remained to be seen whether America was his land of heart's desire.

* * *

The poet unwrapped the oblong package that had arrived insured through the mail. He had to use scissors on the tough tape that sealed the box. As he slit this, a smell of pine oil or some wood fragrance filled the air. The packing, a veritable mummy-case of paper bandages, was like a scented sarcophagus. He lifted out the ginseng capsules, pulled at a paper slip on which was printed an advertisement for comfrey root with pepsin and lobelia with cayenne, though in neither case did the advertisement state the purpose of the remedies. Black cohosh. Mistletoe capsules. He pulled out the big glass jar of natural Vitamin C from rose-hips with citrus bioflavonoids, rutin and hesperidin complex. These were sunshine aids to help with the winter, surely complex enough to deal with the new complex winter of snowflakes and central heating. Lastly, the capsules of valerian root, skullcap, hops and passion flower, drowsy flowers powdered for winter. Hibernation.

* * *

The spirit of the boat tonight — who was it, he or she — romanced the Professor to himself as he wandered through the public rooms. Later, after dinner, at his usual table, watching the dancing, he saw her, a tall woman whose hair was as white as the ship's wake even though she could not have been more than thirty-five or so. She wore a black velvet sheath, a long dress, slashed high up for dancing, and her thigh flashed in the velvet like a wave-crest, a 'white horse' seen from the deck at night in the light of the liner's blazing windows. These were the signs that made the Professor believe he had discerned tonight's habitation or materialization of the spirit of the great liner. It was his belief — no, hypothesis — that just as the consciousness of a man wanders at night in his dreams through the lighted and dark rooms, countries and landscapes of his own sleeping body, so the consciousness of the liner could at certain times every day and night afford to lose hold on the details of its functioning and instead wander, disguised as one of the passengers, through its holds, ballrooms and cabin-spaces. For all he knew, the spirit of the ship could detach itself completely from the vessel and, taking perhaps the form of a white-eyed wave or the great coiling wake (like a twisted umbilicus) the vessel trailed, issue into the ocean and explore the depths and make acquaintance with whatever consciousnesses swam that green gulf. He could not follow the spirit there, however, but in the vessel itself he had noticed that there was some person every night who had attached to him or her a certain imagery, or a glow, that showed they were more than mortal. They were rather the energies of steel plate and turbine, bow wave and stern wake, self-fashioned into human form. One evening a waiter had dropped a pile of clean plates and they had fallen in the lap of a man sitting at a nearby table, striking his knee. All the plates shattered, and the man was non-committal to the waiter's anguished concern. The Professor kept an eye on this man during the meal, since the incident of the plates was not conclusive, the puzzling strength and imperturbability of the leg might have been due to its being artificial, made of steel plate like the hull of the ship — but would that in itself not have made him a suitable receptacle for the spirit? His imperturbability was more indicative. And did the spirit enter certain suitable passengers, or did it create those passengers? And if so, *when* did it create them? In the case of this woman in the black dress had the ship's spirit travelled back through time and entered the semen of the woman's father, preparing her for this voyage from her conception, allowing her the gift of life — perhaps in better health than other, unfavoured mortals — for many years, as a mode of thanks for being the unconscious vessel of the liner's intentions? Might not the liner, having entered this woman, conceive another child, a child that was of the ocean knowledgeable, as true and as faithful as the schedules of an ocean liner, of such broad emotion that it could unite the shores of the Atlantic in common understanding, and as strong as oil power and steelplate?

The Professor now made a practice of encountering those he had discriminated as such vessels of the spirit. He was not much of a dancer, but he would risk the ship's displeasure at this, so he got up and asked the white-haired woman for a dance. She seemed pleased, and they set out on their quickstep. She was an excellent dancer:

> When you do dance, I wish you
> A wave o' th Sea, that you might ever do
> Nothing but that: move still, still so:
> And owne no other Function.

and since the Professor was a receptive man and a quick learner, they got on very well. They danced several times, and when the Professor bade his new friend good night with a smiling handshake, she leaned her head forward and kissed him on the cheek, with an equal warmth. The Professor went to his solitary cabin, very pleased by this encounter with the liner, within the liner. He sat down at the small writing desk and wrote up his notes.

At breakfast the young white-haired woman was puzzled and hurt. She smiled at her friend of last night from her table, but he stared coldly at her and turned away, sat down, opened a small black book and began writing in it. Perhaps, she thought, she had been too quick to show her pleasure in the dance, and it was a man's world, and he was a Professor in it. A pity. She spread some butter on thin toast and forgot about the Professor. Who was not worried. He had discerned the morning hypostasis of the ship's spirit in a small elderly man clothed in white he had met on the promenade deck, very freckled with age, but most intelligent to talk with, as he would expect the ship's spirit to be. Apart from the elderly man's insistence that he had never taken this voyage before, it was an agreeable half-hour. The Professor lived in hopes of becoming an avatar himself. He could not imagine what the sensation would be like. He hoped he would remain conscious, like the possessed Voodoo priests with their quality of *la prise des yeux* holding on to their watching eyes even though the gods rode their necks. After all, had he not made more serious, amorous encounter with the spirit of the liner once? He had not been able to find that lady again, and her cabin was always locked.

* * *

The library's windows open on the lake. The lake's windows open on the library. The lake's librarians walk on the library's terraces; startle the gentle creatures and they melt away, dribble away through the paving-stone cracks, leaving only small wet footmarks.

* * *

The liner floats on the waves like a large closed volume, its covers tooled in black and white. The sea keeps plucking at its pages but so far has not read it. The sea would like to become acquainted with the ship's contents, the ship sinking lop-sided down through the waves fitfully illuminated by its bursting boilers, and send its fishes to nuzzle through the staterooms, but so far the liner has displayed only its title — *SS Messenger* — proudly as it speeds like an inter-library loan between Goode Olde England and the Great Universal States. Perhaps the spirit of the liner read its manifest to the spirit of the Atlantic while the rest of us slept.

The sirens called us out to our emergency stations by the lifeboats for our boat drill. We had lifted the little trap-doors in the wardrobes to find the clumsy stiff orange jackets, and with difficulty we followed the printed instructions that showed us how to wear the lifejackets correctly so that even if flung into the sea unconscious we would float in our ballgowns watery with diamonds with nose and mouth out into the air, so that the sea would not become too thoroughly acquainted with our contents. Now we stood in groups lumpishly dressed in the horrible non-fitting gear, deprived of human form, the children among us blowing shrill whistles and falling over and having to be helped up because with those things on they *rolled* submitting ourselves to the ministrations of the sharp-eyed purser and his master-at-arms, a steel-eyed petty officer, who did not care if we was paying customers or not we had to wear lifejackets as trimly and correctly as him and his staff by bugger; and meanwhile the orchestra stood aside like inhabitants of another world on their platform fiddling with their instruments, couthly and slimly dressed, taking no part or notice as if they were all merely notes of music and could in the event of a disaster detach themselves and float calmly away over the sea; or they would play us hypnotically down into the water with sprightly and serious hymns, their bubbles bursting in music, uncaring; or, at the last moment when the brine lapped at the plate glass doorway of the first class ballroom, lead the piping procession up on to the deck and at the end when they had seen us musically installed in our lifeboats in beaming rows simply pour themselves by breathing out more thoroughly than usual through their instruments (the fiddler has his fiddle-raft) and float away as a complex pattern of vibrations to some station where they can be reconstituted by the musicians union.

* * *

The only time I ever lost my memory, said the ship's doctor, was during a storm at sea. It was a whopper — force nine, a graduate hurricane — and most of the passengers were down with seasickness. I give an injection for that now, of course, and there I was running hither and thither with my little bright needle, seeing the mess people had got themselves into, not knowing how to stow their possessions, you see, everything was tossed higgledy-piggledy by the rocking ship, the bathrooms were all leaking, foul with spilled toothpowder and talcum and mouth-wash and broken glass, in the staterooms the wardrobe doors kept snapping open and the drawers in the dressing tables sliding open and spilling their contents out, and there in the centre of it all a human creature that I had to comfort and inject, in bedclothes looking as tempest-tossed as the outside turmoil. I saw three hundred people in eighteen hours and at the end of that time I was (like everybody else) going about my job automatically and robot-like. The other doctor is a drinker and smoker, and therefore quite safe from mental trouble, until he dies from drink and smoke. I had to take time off sick to see him, since my mind was full of waves and rumpled bedlinen, and I had forgotten my own name, and what ship this was, said the doctor.

* * *

Before launching the ship they should send in flames down the launching-rails a full-sized replica in plywood and balsa wood painted in as dazzling white and black as the mother ship; maybe they should send out as many of these votive ships to burn on the moonlit waters as the liner is to take voyages. After this number of voyages, the mother-ship should be scrapped and rebuilt, no matter what. Though some might argue that to send out a votive ship before each voyage, rather than announcing the great addition of voyages in one, might be as propitious.

These votive ships would be seen after their deaths-by-fire escorting the solid liner through storms and battles: like wraiths painted in St Elmo's Fire; serene pulsating blue companions on the night sea, invisible in the. daytime but suspected in the bending patterns of waves. Truly, the votive ships should be manned with a full complement of crew and officers in painted uniforms stuffed with straw, and these wraiths will hail distressed vessels with warnings and navigational instructions.

The votive ships have been seen by the astronauts, like fiery ghosts plying between the earth and the moon; ghost-carriers full of Viet-Cong souls.

* * *

He thought American students a talented bunch. In this university there was no worry about money, many had rich parents. So talent had a chance. Some abilities went with a well-heeled life. Languages, for example. Many students spoke several languages since their parents had summer holiday houses in those countries. French was widely spoken. Proust had been read.

Abilities that went with an untroubled budget were not the only ones, though. He was discussing a Dylan Thomas poem, 'When I Was Young and Easy', in a tutorial with a young man, that is, not in class, but privately in his office. They were discussing how rhythms of this author's poems commanded and compelled, and thought that the cause of it here was a rolling anapaestic line, when the student suddenly began to utter a setting of the poem. He sung it easily and sweetly with not a trace of the formal rhythm, but instead a haunting, contemplative sound. He sung it so easily and sweetly for his teacher, looking him in the eye and smiling as he did so, that the poem and the boy took up entirely changed feelings. A door had opened on a sweet and pleasing existence in which the strenuous examination of texts had no place, and yet only the people who insisted on that — the professors — were at all damaged. Dinosaurs of the academy contrived curricula, while the young people took only what worked for them, what the genius in them told them was true. Quite unselfconsciously this six-foot twenty-year-old had given his teacher a fresh view not only of the poem — he remembered how Dylan Thomas himself read it with the face of a drowned man, bolt-eyed and puffed with drink, and the voice of an organ, which was his unconquerable gift — but of America also. The line 'a man of fortune greeting heirs' came into his head, was that of it? Were these people going to grow up with thus such a sweet and natural relationship to the poetic forces within them; or was this a brief flowering natural to the age twenty among all men at all times? He had felt a physical stirring as the young man sang; the latter could have seduced him with his song; though at other times his fatherhood had been stirred by sweet and natural actions from his own sons.

* * *

She had lost her quartz stone. They had made love on her sofa, discarded clothes all over the room, and when they got up and separated their garments, they could not find her pendant with the glittering stone fastened to it. 'I will buy you another and better one, he said gallantly, but she would not be comforted and her afterglow turned to irritation. 'My Dear,' he said, 'that great stone always looked to me like your wisdom; often when I did not know you as I do now I would glance at the great stone hanging at your throat and I would say to myself "That is she, collector of light, many faceted distributor of light." Now we have made love together the stone has somehow evaporated; we shall find it together; it is like a dew that has melted in the daytime; even now it is forming again in some secret place; perhaps within you somewhere.' But nothing he could say, nor his love, would compensate her for the loss of her stone. She had had it from her teacher; she believed it had magic powers, for she could look into it as it twirled on the end of its chain and doing so brought vivid and logically interesting pictures to her reveries. Now it was gone. She sent him away crossly; when he had left the room and the flat she set about taking up the carpets and moving furniture to find her stone.

The steward took her cases and barged open the stateroom door with them. 'There you are Miss,' and turned away before she could give him a tip. She realized that tips — hefty ones — were expected when the voyage was over, and that meanwhile there was a pretence of disinterested service, gladly and freely given, by highly paid crew members not concerned with gratuities, but only in keeping the passengers happy. She loved the stateroom with its light wood and its fitted furniture, the tiny bathroom tucked neatly behind the entrance to the cabin. She began to unpack her nighties and other best things, hanging them up in the cupboard. She felt something fall out of the front of her dress, and lie glittering on her night-clothes. It was her quartz pendant! How had it got there, was it caught all that time in a seam of this dress? But it had been to the cleaners! At any rate it was back, and she was free from *that* lover, whom she privately suspected of having actually purloined this quartz and crystalline portion of her identity. But that was not so, and she had found it again, and that made her very happy. She would look into it after her bath, maybe it would tell her its adventures. She wound up her rather dressy small gold wristwatch and went in for her bath.

* * *

The ship's doctor was holding forth playfully in several voices to his assistant about the first-class passengers. 'The smoky, fruity tones of the French horn,' said Alicia, reclining among the silver bowls of dusky grapes, 'overload me, I'm afraid, until I am a complete spectacle, rather like this' with a quick gesture she tossed the rosewater and floating petals out of a silver fingerbowl, so that the liquid splashed on the rug and spattered darkly a silk-covered cushion at her feet, 'listen . . .' With a wet forefinger she traced a hum from the rim of the bowl, high, thrumming, something between a hum and a squeak, like the cicada trees. 'I feel in those moments like a tree on whose leaves the cicadas trill,' with a quick smile and tossing her long white hair over the red sofa-back, 'Herbert, kiss me while my lips are still trilling.' 'You thrum deliciously Alicia,' mumbled Herbert, on his knees in full evening dress, crushing his cigar out in a bowl full of grapes, or a fresh dish of mayonnaise . . . those first class passengers . . . do you know how much they pay for a cruise in the Caribbean?' 'Thirty thou.' 'That's right. Thirty thousand *pounds*. That immunizes them against nothing. I once had one of them open for a gall-bladder. Exactly the same as anybody else. A good thing we're all alike under the skin. The ultimate millionaire would have his personalized anatomical atlas printed, with any peculiarities compiled by his personal physician. Gold-plated scalpels. That reminds me . . .' The ship's doctor decided not to mention the small watch he had found inside the school mistress's death-incision, the cut that had let the air out of her. Instead he told the purser, who requested a written report. It was a lie that they had the murderer behind bars. They were hoping that he would give himself up before the ship docked at New York, otherwise the whole voyage of passengers would have to be kept in the ship for interrogation. There were fifteen hundred passengers on the liner, all told. And into any one of them the red spirit of murder could have entered. Meanwhile, enquiries were proceeding discreetly both on board and by ship's radio. Instant dismissal was the reward if a whisper of this reached any of the passengers, and the company directors did not exclude the Captain from this order.

* * *

Opulent archives in the lake, in the towers of the library. In the gardens of the library wet footprints. A bush of red berries that are replete mosquitoes. A bush of claws that are the plant's leaves. A ruined room with the river running through the end of it, but that is in England. The fly snatched at his sleeve. The guilt of that little murder may have infected every person that travelled on the vessel. It was as though the spirit of the liner had been summarily dismissed by means of blade. How it would wing its way upwards, the great black and white liner sprouting gold wings and heaving off the sea's surface, plucking its great keel out of the waves and rowing off into heaven, a dark speck against the moon. Meanwhile the ghostless substructure of spiritless metal and electricity left behind merely dragged its way to New York. Had anybody told? Had the murderer been caught? Had the liner! s spirit entered the body of some uninspired policeman and dedicated him to feats of detection? Only a little murder of a school-teacher with an itchy cunt and a big quartz pendant. But the strict black and white galleries cried out for blood! The sea turned into blood that clotted into bloodbergs that softly stank and clung so that until a tiny figure — whether man or woman he couldn't tell — ran out on to the deck and cried, 'I did it — take me,' the great clotted screws of the ship coiling a bloody taffy could take them no further. The tiny murderous figure stands there, mouth calling, a black blot in a white face like a hole in a star, and as the confession echoes in the Atlantic air the seas with a sigh turn white and clear once again, uniformed figures escort their murderer below decks, and the liner resumes its spanking speed through sparkling waters to the tall lighted windows of New York.

* * *

The cicadas in the trees, the Gorgon's whistle, running down the scale as the walker nears, great beings, singing and sweating in their sleep, a steel shaving factory, a tent of invisible lathes, a lookout post, an amused observer that falls silent as you wonder, begins to whistle like a kettle as you walk away, can you catch him out, he is not humming, not he, as you swing around, the humming is coming from that tree, no that over there or is it the wire on the dead tree, the telegraph pole, is it a transformer or radio static, is it the eternity drone, the tree playing its raga, a sob like a song, like tuning into silence, it fades because it goes where you can no longer listen, you cannot follow this music, there it is across the lake all the trees on this side have fallen silent, and then once again you are midway in the pattern of the noise, or it sings and you walk into the song, then it falls silent companionably so that you may get used to the sound before it begins again and you are a part of the new song, tuned in, and you can see by the way the tremblings run across the lake, making the library blur and shake, in the mirror-library the books are all worth reading, they are tuned into silence, there, look in the water, a mirror librarian is walking backwards out of the swing doors. The cicada song in the maples made you see that by kindly adjusting its shrill song to your desires, they are wooden trunks which are already doors to new worlds without the benefit of chopping, planing, fitting, wardrobes of new clothes, banks of a green or golden money, they are one of the three universities on this campus: Brick and Mortar College, Lake University and the School of Singing Trees. Ah there is the Professor of Arboreal Urinology sniffing at the roots of that Song, and ah, he is about to teach a Freshman bitch on the front lawn how to clasp and walk on six staggering legs while barking with excellent joy.

* * *

Death kept on coming for him like a great black and white ship lined with red, red plush walls, red carpets, red mirrors, red engines run on red oil. The crew and officers dressed in red jacket and trousers with little red ties and red badges of office difficult to see against the other reds. He encountered this death glaring straight at me. Her clothes surmounted by a feather hat were lying in a heap on the floor. I was astonished and frightened. With more courage than I thought was in me, I groped through the dark until I felt the wooden scrolled sofa-end, and I felt down it with my hands. There was nobody there. The sofa was empty, just covered with littered typescript. A page had fallen across the typewriter cover on the floor. I found a torch and looked round the room, shaking a little. No visitor. I went back to the switches and tried them again. The fuses were still out. Then the lightning came again and I saw the nude lady glaring at me from the sofa. I leapt through the door, slamming it behind me. I had left the torch behind.

'I lit a candle in the kitchen, found the whiskey-bottle and poured myself a nip. Then shielding my flame with the palm of my hand, I crept back along corridor and quietly turned the handle. Inside the room lit only by the candle, I raised my eyes to where I had seen the lady. She was still there, but now she was smiling. A flash of lightning, and I saw her clearly again. Now she was glaring as before. This time I kept steady without quailing. And when my eyes, which showed the after-image of a black lady with glaring white eyeballs floating wherever I looked, had recovered and adjusted themselves to candle-light again, I raised my candle and saw how the lady's form changed as the light shifted, and how she was made of pages of typescript scattered on a sofa with their shading and grey message, and her hat the typewriter case, her clothes its shadow, and its brave feather a MS page that had lodged upright. I thought of how people looked at pages before reading them; I saw that I had truly stepped back from my work, and I remembered then the title of the flung piece I had been engaged on. It was a semi-popular article about German baroque virgins, the wooden sculpture of the late middle ages that had been made so still in a time of constant warfare, famine, and military brutality. I had called this piece, "Still Lady in Anger."'

* * *

The great water-tree of the world with its roots in caverns measureless and stalactited, and its foliage capturing thunder first of all in the gardens of the English sea-college. There he was walking along the flowering garden paths considering the green fingers that had won the Britain-in-Bloom competition for the last five years running, when he heard a call from somewhere above his head, 'Ahoy there! You in the garden! Ahoy! He looked round him puzzled for he knew the garden was usually empty in the early afternoon, and he paused, for there was a jovial urgency in the cry which seemed pleasant. 'Ahoy!' Then he lifted his eyes and thought he must have wandered nearer the road than he had realized, for there, surely, was the new block of flats. But then he realized that the tiers of windows rising above his head were all round, like portholes, and the apartment block was slowly gliding from left to right towards him as he watched. 'Ahoy there!' He tilted his head and took off his hat and saw for the first time the size of the thing. A smart red-dressed figure was leaning over the highest rail and calling him with a megaphone. He cocked his head to the call and took an involuntary step forward, then a perspiration swept him as he saw a breeches buoy made of red cord and canvas swinging slowly down the black-and-white side of the ship. His hand came up and wiped his forehead and pushed forward as if to wave and then changed as if to shove the sight away, 'No . . .' He turned then away from the ship and found that his feet could scarcely lift from the ground but with effort he broke into a stumbling run. 'Ahoy . . .' faded, over his shoulder he saw the stern of the great ship trailing a coiling wake like a bleeding birth-string with a great rasping through the boughs and twigs of the trees. He saw a holly-bush crushed under the margins of the thing, he saw water foaming white under the turf which was slowly sealing up as he watched. The road at the end of the gardens slowly came into view and he heard a long trailer lorry grinding up the hill. He was able to forget the visitation with the help of this lorry which, or so he persuaded himself, might easily have given him a feverish vision of death; they were known at the time as 'juggernauts' and were held responsible for many accidents on the motorways.

One evening he had been working late over his books in the library. A class bell rang — perhaps by short-circuit, classes had long since finished for the day — and he looked up from the table and his manuscript; for a long moment relished the lights of the library reflecting in the great lake. He noticed then that the lights were all circular and the colour of them was red, and that they towered higher than the great willow trees. A lifeboat was being lowered over the side of the vessel on lengthening red cables, and as he watched, touched the lake water. No ripples blurred the reflections. It cast free; in a ruddy glow he could see figures bending over their oars and a slim white figure in the stern-sheets like a coxswain. He rose from the table clutching his manuscript and swung the window open on to the library terrace. Slowly he walked out as the lifeboat reached the shore, the oars were shipped, and the coxswain stepped nimbly ashore. 'Ahoy!' she called, and he felt himself step towards her down the terrace stairs, but then he stopped because he saw all the library windows opening and many people stepping out of the windows, some in modern dress, some dressed in fashions of bygone times, and each with a book or books clutched under his or her arm. As he watched, the spirits left the library in cheerful talkative groups and boarded the lifeboat, that seemed no fuller for its freight, nor were the reflections troubled, nor did the water rise on its sides. He started forward but as he came closer he saw that the woman was nude, and had a wound in her right side, high up on the abdomen. He stopped in fear. The woman turned sadly away and stepped into the boat, pushing the shore away as she stepped, and the lowered oars glowed red in the lake water. One by one the portholes went out, and the library reappeared in the lake. He was at the library table, and the books in that reflected library were as much good to him as their originals, for when he glanced at one before him on the table, preparatory to closing it up and putting it away, he found that he could not understand the type. He took his pocket-mirror out of his briefcase: the book was printed in mirror-writing. So was that book, and this: he had read about this condition: the nerve-pathways to the hemispheres of the brain reversed spontaneously, or as a result of prolonged emotional stress, and the person afflicted became his mirror-self, his own doppelganger.

* * *

The great shed of the theatre with its many windows was dark and deserted. I inserted my secret key into the bolts of the glass front door, and slipped inside. There were no lights on. The lobby in its gilt and carving looked beaten up, antique, like a weathered ship's figure-head. The booking office window was sealed by a shutter, like a drum with its skin. I eased open the stalls door, and pushed my way carefully, without panic, through the heavy velvet curtains hung to hinder drafts and noise during performances. There was enough light from the roof-lantern for me to see dimly the repeated rows of seats, all empty, arranged in horseshoes rows, and the stage itself with its curtain up, and shrouded shapes disposed on its boards in the gloom. I walked carefully down the aisle and mounted the steps at the side of the orchestra pit. I recognized the shapes on the stage — the two padded cells were set up! Each was a cage of wooden bars painted to resemble iron, and each had its set of padding to fit the sides and floor, a wadded substance sewn into canvas that buckled on to the cage sides. There was a door to the cage, and a small barred hatch also, to enable the guard or keeper to roll a commode into the cell for the prisoner to use in his saner moments. It was one of the great features of this new play that not only was the word 'shit' much used during it, but there was a noted scene in which the padding was removed after one of the principal's seizures revealing him and his cell liberally daubed with a brown paste (this, on the analogy of the horror make-up man's 'Kensington Gore' in England, was known as 'Tennessee Turd', in homage to the famous American playwright). After the seizure, and this was the climax to the play, the madman was shown standing among this detested shambles, quite cured. There was much conversation during the play between the mad pair, companionably seated on their respective commodes. The cast also included three guards and a woman psychiatrist. The guards, at first shocked by the prisoners' unembarrassed use of the commodes, learned a freedom of speech from the madmen on the potties, and a relaxation of prejudice, while the villain of the piece was the male analyst of the lady doctor in charge, and he never appeared on stage. Whenever the lady learnt relaxation in her approach to the disorders of her patients, it was time for her analysis, and she returned from the senior doctor even worse than before, critical, full of blame. I had thought from time to time that a better climax to the play would be to imitate the old stage pantomime slapstick routine of the comic decorators. Clumsy with their paint these skilled clowns gradually involve several orders of people of increasing dignity and taboo in their rainbow paint-wars, all becoming identically dressed in coloured splashes: first the gardener, then the grocery boy, then the milkman, then the butler, then the vicar, with the climax of the greatest untouchable of them all, the lady of the house with her French maid returning from a shopping expedition laden with parcels. This unfortunate pair would open the door at exactly the most inopportune moment and receive more paint than all the rest put together, in this brotherhood, sisterhood of clumsiness, non-elegance, and metamorphosis of one into another with joyous and amazed shouts. I thought this play should end by the whole cast pelting the lady psychiatrist with Tennessee Turds, and her terrible old analyst dying of a heart attack offstage with a great muffled cry. Then the lady joins in the battle and rolls in the dung with the rest in amazed joy — all cured. But the public was not ready for that. Nor could I discuss the matter with the Captain of the liner at cocktails. 'I saw one of your plays once on TV, Mr Umph. Strong meat, I thought, but fascinating.' Thus being blunt, nautical, and pleasing the customers at one and the same time; with the little brown gnome in its white jacket springing up with a fresh clear gin tinkling like a deleterious alarm clock at his elbow.

I sat down on one of the commodes, and took one of the non-odorous plasticine-like sticks of Tennessee Turd from the box and rolled it meditatively between my fingers. It softened as I rolled and it took the heat of my body. I found this very conducive to thought. Then suddenly the lights went up and Alicia's voice blared from the wings, 'Portrait of the great playwright haunting a smash hit!' I turned, and without rising from my throne, flung my length of brown putty at the voice. The lady psychiatrist in my mind, in my play, laughed aloud at the joke so precisely illustrated: anal-ist. (In England, theatrical shit is known as 'Larry Squitters'.)

* * *

There are devices sold here that turn off the porthole of television automatically if you have fallen asleep watching it. I thought at first that this was fun, that young couples would snuggle up and make love during the scary bits in the late late horror show, or allow 'Mission Impossible' to merge with their post coital reveries. 'The Monster is coming,' yells the great mad psychiatrist. Indeed, the Monster is coming. It's *blood* Sir. What is *blood* doing on your stairs? I might ask you the same question, my love, your period is very early this month.

But now I think of lonely old people who cannot sleep, but only doze, or who fall asleep inadvertently, who cannot afford the electricity if the house runs on while they are sleeping. And I think of the dutiful son, having seen that the parental money is properly invested, or that the tiny annuity provides for the necessities of life; as a final fondness fitting automatic devices to the household so that the lights left on or the television left flickering at the end of the programme — dawn — will not drain the resources of that annuity. I see this dutiful son closing the front door for the last time as he leaves for his job in Tennessee. The lonely parent remaining is pleased also, since nothing could be more undignified and unpropitious for the after-life than to be discovered stone cold dead with open eyes in front of 'To Catch a Thief' or rotting while next Fall's unique programme of spy films rapidly approaches.

I was intrigued by the fashion of printing slogans on one's clothes. I had tee-shirts stencilled for myself, and wore them to rehearsals of that filthy play about madness I'm starring in, they pronounced from my chest in great syllables written in packing-case letters like some great mantram standing between the tits, to which all. thoughts were attracted, or some minor Zahir. I had written on me: COSMO DESPAIR; VOTE FOR THE MONOCEROS BROS; I AM DEAD DO NOT WAKE ME; I AM INVISIBLE YOU CANNOT SEE THIS; SHRIEK AT FATE; THE WOMB DISCLOSES; PEACHES ARE UNCHANGED; DEATH CAME FOR ME THROUGH THE TV SET; LET ME BE YOUR APERIENT; and many others. Eventually our author (God save the mark — GOD SAVE THE MARK) forbade this mute interference with his dialogue from my lettered chest.

When our show goes on television, as the programme time comes near, I shall think of the television audience as an immense ocean liner approaching us, studded with millions of portholes. Each porthole has its viewer and somewhere, down there near the water-line, is the flickering glass of my old dad's set. I wave to him but he cannot wave back. The ocean is bathed in the flickering colours of TV, but the liner for the main part is an ancient black-and-white set much carved, scrolled, beaded, and curlicued, like some ancient storytelling machine. 'That's my old dad, sailing out of sight,' I cry when our play is over and our story fading, 'That's the American TV nation sailing out of sight!'

* * *

In the glass cottage they could feel the tide in the stone, as the needle fragments in the granite aligned together, pointing like compass needles or exclamation marks of amazement at the moon as it rolled overhead, rolled through the underworld. 'Don't we have to start our packing soon,' she said from the bath, 'can we just close the place up and have Giles look after it, and take as little as possible to America?' 'I'll need some books and a jacket, those are the only heavy things.' He came in in his pyjamas and sat on the edge of the bath. 'I don't want that missing owner coming back while we're away and taking possession.' 'That my dear is a fantasy. He was legally presumed dead., and in any case the cottage was deeded to the man who sold it to us. Giles will air it and Mary will dust it.' 'I can't help feeling that we've but rented it, and one day the owner will come and take it away from us. I wish it would take us over the ocean like the ship, and set down somewhere convenient for work on the other side.' 'I can just imagine the Captain of the liner watching with empurpled brow the small glass cottage overtake his spanking great liner on the high seas, and leave him rocking behind in its wake. Or better still, to have a Boscastle door and an American door, and just walk in and out of the Glass Cottage wherever we please, as though our home extended behind all space.' 'And time too?' 'And time too, though I think we'd need proper weapons to, protect us.' 'Is there any truth that the cottage was once a church?' 'Or a hermitage by a stream, and the owner could trace It back in the family to Cornish saints? You still feel like an interloper?' 'No. I think it's still a Church.' 'Used for sex.' 'Used for sex.' The stream, like liquid electricity, flickered In the sun outside, flowing under the broad green leaves of the dock plant.

* * *

The man in the drab coat approached, and gripped the Professor's arm. 'I believe you have killed a woman, Sir, and it is my duty to arrest you.' 'I killed no woman, Inspector. I sunk a liner, I sunk it in flame with myself and 1499 other people on board. But I never killed the woman who loved me.' 'That is the crime you did not commit, Professor, the 1499 people are safe, and now I am subtracting you.' 'That leaves 1498 people to ready themselves for death,' cried the Professor wildly. 'Look, there is the liner you said I sunk,' he gesticulated towards the trees surrounding the lake, 'and there is the woman you say I killed, they have come to take me away from this godawful country,' cried the Professor running down the grass slope towards the water, tripping and falling full length asprawl. As he lay he bit his arm as hard as he could, the tweed of his jacket was rough and dry in his mouth; he waited for the man to grab his body and lift him to his feet. Nobody came. After a while he struggled to his knees and looked around. There was nobody within sight, though a person sitting at a library window might well have seen him fall. He patted his jacket pocket to see whether the hand-mirror he kept there for his reading was secure and unbroken. He felt that he had fallen head-first into some book, and that he could not read except in mirror writing because he was staring from the white page, from the other side of the horizontal bars of print, as though he were in some padded cell. The mirror was intact. He had resigned himself to incidents such as the encounter with the arresting policeman. So long as he did not fling himself about and cause himself injury, he was quite safe, he thought. Unless the arresting policeman happened to be real, and there must be simple tests for ascertaining the reality of policemen, as of librarians, looking down at the feet of the tall stout man who brought his books, and making certain that the man left no wet footmarks on the linoleum floor as he walked away.

* * *

I drink at Glastonbury
from Joseph's well, I pluck
a water-flower in my hands
that springs from the long
coppery-tasting roots of water
winding below the hills and through
the flowers and thorns. The bossed
roofs of the churches repeat it
and the knots
tied at head and feet
of the peaceful likeness of the
reclining stone bishop: much comes
to rest in that water-flower.

The two lay at rest in the water-flower in the glass cottage. The roots of the water-flower stretched along the walls and down behind them deep into the ground, where they fastened to the great straight root that ran to the roots in the great hill reservoir. The stem of the water-flower ran down beneath the bath and beneath the ground also, but gathered anastomosis as it travelled beneath the roads until it met the great sewer-stem that branched and flowered into the ocean. The roots were above them, the branches below, and they lay at rest in one of the clear bellflowers of water that budded along these vines. They lay as though at the bottom of the sea, stretched out in Davy Jones' locker. They could feel, or thought they could feel, in their clear soapless water, the rains prickle gently on the hills, the rains that had fitted themselves together into the reservoir, and the tide of the sea that pulled all waters with it. It was an altar of the water-church, or a peaceful tomb of the same communion. If they did indeed one day lie at the bottom of the sea's branches, bedded in sea-flesh of ooze, skeletons full of windows through which the sea-life swum, the moist-air currents fashioning the great stem from which the white clouds budded and the clear rain fruited, all the water of the world would flow past the bones of the lovers, and this water-shrine of pleasure was good practice for that state of being. 'One thousand black-coated clergymen are at this moment raising me to their lips and gargling with me in preparation for their Sunday sermon,' she said, 'And in an hour's time they will reject jugs of me for the bottled variety with a little colouring and some alcohol. That will be the Spanish branch of my corpse.' 'People have died before,' he said, 'and been drowned. And their bodies have entered the whole world, just as ours does.' 'We were made of them to begin with,' she replied, 'and I did not say we do not have companions in our good fortune.' The sea entered their rooms which dissolved like sugar and became green slowly beating caverns larger than America and England combined, their bones rolled in the knowledge that was coming to them as they touched, and penetrated, and lay in the water-flower like the world, and the seeds of it. The water grew cold swiftly and she got out, put on a towelling dressing gown and boiled water for coffee while he got dressed. 'Where did these barnacles on the mirror come from', he called laughing. 'Pull the other one,' she called back, 'it's got sea-slugs on it.'

* * *

The Willaparks was the grassy bluff that rose to the south of Boscastle; the sea-cliff thatched with turf and breaking away to sheer cliffs into the sea. You walked towards the harbour, a very Aegean appearance, with a long pier of big, square blocks of stone shutting off the mouth of the bay and leaving a narrow gap for the fishing vessels, that at low tide lay all around tilted on the coarse sand. You climbed along the path to the left, which gave a very fine view of the great stone that dominated the bay, a peninsula that the sea would in another few centuries convert into a true islet. For how many thousands of years before the reign of that monarch this stone had resembled a sculpture of the widowed Queen Victoria, nobody but a geologist could have surmised, but the resemblance was so striking, with the snub nose and the uptilted chin, the headdress and the little veil, that one wondered that the seagulls dare sit on it and scream at it as they wheeled about. Most of them indeed preferred the truly isolated boulder, white as a wedding cake with their feathered bodies and their droppings, that lay further out to seaward; at one time this must have made another arm to protect the land; now the stone pier and the rearing head were the two interdigitating redoubts of defence, and the linking stem of the head's peninsula was deeply burrowed by the persistent sea. At all high tides one could hear the regular booming of the waves, the shock under the feet as the water struck the walls of underground caverns; at low tide the entrance to one of these caves was visible, in regular pulses spuming white into the green from an entrance the size of a small railway tunnel.

Queen Victoria stared directly at the Willaparks. The Willaparks stared back with a deep, a very deep and sheer cleft in the rocks where the sea was separating *them* from the land. The climb up on to the grassy cliff where the white coastguard station perched was not severe, the path had a gentle slope, and there were seats placed for a full view of Queen Victoria. The woman who lived in the Glass Cottage had climbed up there today specifically to think about Queen Victoria, and widowhood, and the lot of women in the world, and there was a silly little tune going through her head 'since you were not married you are not a widow, no need for sorrow, no need for sorrow'. The Glass Cottage would have to be given up, sold, and she would have to return to London to work, probably as a secretary or teacher. She sat and watched the white wave pump out of the cliff tunnel again and again, and could raise no emotion about her loss, it was too great. The move was beginning to worry her, and she wondered if she could cope with London, but apart from that it was all apathy. 'Probably,' she thought, 'because he was drowned at sea, and there was no funeral to help me mourn.' So she sat instead and stared at the natural effigy of the widowed Queen, and tried to feel bereaved. The white wave shunted again and again out of the tunnel in Victoria's flank, with the noise of trains and with a distant thunder, it was like a white door in the black cliff, or like lightning in a black cloud. A little squall blew across the bay towards her, roughening the waves and producing with the fitful sun a brief column of bright coiling colours, and dashed against the cliff and vanished. She got up from the seat, deciding she would walk up and across the Willaparks to Forrabury Church, and find the Sound there. At the top of the path she turned left, inland, where the cultivated strips were — almost the only place in Britain where strip-farming had survived — and started along the green path. As she walked Forrabury Church Tower rose out of the land, out of the small dip that had concealed it. On the long straight path the turf grew very short and implanted with moss. She did not know the reason for this, unlike the other path, it had not been constructed with gravel and sand, but simply grew, or perhaps the sheep nibbled it. The path gave no sound of footsteps; she glided. Coming towards her was a tall woman wearing an immense white hat that deeply shaded her face. The woman from the Glass Cottage stepped to one side with a polite smile as they passed, she could not clearly see the other woman's face, and was startled when the other shot out an arm and gripped her by the wrist, and began to draw her closer. 'Child,' she said, 'look.' The young woman felt a sudden pain in her side and saw herself stretched out on a small white bed. A woman in a uniform carrying pails came through the door, caught her hand to her mouth. 'Look.' She saw herself sliding a key into the lock of a shabby flat. 'Look.' She saw herself walking under foreign trees bearing enormous catkins. 'Look.' She saw herself taking her bath in the Glass Cottage, but it was not with her dead lover, it was with another, darker man. 'Do not leave the Glass Cottage, you will receive the death due to another woman at a madman's hand.' 'Who are you?' She woke to herself in Forrabury Church, the tall woman was holding her hand and they were standing at the font as if it was an altar. The church was perfectly silent, as if attentive. The woman slid the wooden lid off the font, dipped her finger in the water, signed her forehead with it, signed the young woman's. The water was icy cold, or burning, it seemed to go right through to the back of her head. Her womb gave a great thump, a shudder that made her see white for a moment like sea spuming from a tunnel cave with the whole fetch of the Celtic Ocean behind it, and she staggered back feeling for the support of a pew. 'What is your name?' she said, and then the twining wires inside her head darkened as something like a great flock of swallows settled on them with a beautiful chirruping, high and silvery. She felt wetness on her chest and realized that she had been crying so copiously as to darken the collar and front of her blouse. She was sitting and her legs were stiff, the church was dark and she had no idea how long she had been sitting there. The singing in the silence had returned. She thought of her lover, but a new emotion was there, it was as though she could see that he had passed through the world leaving a wake of energy, and the world was better for it, and she could feel in herself the energy that he left, like the wake left by a superb ship plying between two shores. She walked with a firmer step to the church door. As she stepped out into the little diamond-shaped graveyard she stopped astonished. The Willaparks were spread out in front of her in the light of sunset with beauty that she had never seen before, every blade of grass distinct, every tree, every cloud itself and no other, passing for a moment through the world, as she was. She felt that there was such a tale to each one of them, and this tale told the truth, but there was no sadness in the way things and people left their track across the world, like a signature of what they were. She would call these tales 'The Tales of Willa' after Willa's Parks in which she first saw them, and she would write them in the Glass Cottage. She realized that the great head of the Queen at the harbour's entrance was and always had been Willa's head. She realized whose face the dark shadow under the white hat had also been.

* * *

The tumbler spelt out; LET THE LITTLE BLACK GIRL TAKE THE PENCIL. The little black girl, who was actually Persian, giggled at this, and they swept the alphabet aside and found some large sheets of writing paper headed with its drawing of the liner like an address, and sat her down in front of it, and gave her a ball-point, and sat and folded their arms and looked expectant.

The Professor was there, and the poet, the playwright and the actor, the ship's doctor and the school-teacher who was about to die, the fat man was present, and the dapper elderly gentleman with age-freckles like tea-stains in a tablecloth all over his face and brow and even his eyes, was there, but simply to observe. It was late, nearly dawn, and a feeling began which said that it was just about time to finish up, and this had started with the sweeping-away of the letters. The Persian girl — rumoured to be a princess — sat doodling on the paper. Having been chosen she wanted, she said, to give it a chance at least. She doodled slats on squares. Then she doodled cubes, that opened, with lids. Then she doodled cubes with bars, and dark squashy lengths of Tennessee Turd, to tease the playwright. Then she doodled a deep, deep hole, with crosswise removable slats across it. Then her lines got rounder and more life-like, and she doodled a flattened face, that looked as though it was squashed against glass and that finished the page, so she turned over and doodled winged lines. She looked sleepy and intent, and the great diamond on her dusky finger doodled fine lines of focus and refraction across her page. The winged lines became winged serpents which became winged lions with deep, deep mouths, they formed a procession between winged pillars. Then she drew a fleet of winged ships, sailing under a sky with a deep hole shining in it. She drew a blank face with horns, and she put a plus sign at the tip of one horn, and a minus sign to the other one. Then she filled in the blank face with the playwright's face, to tease him. But the work was coming thick and fast now, and her breath was drawing deeply and fast. ASHTAROTH she wrote and I AM THE SEA. I AM THE SUN she wrote and the first bars of a golden dawn shot across the sea and streaked the deck. WHERE IS THE LINER'S SPIRIT she wrote and at this the Professor looked thoughtful — he had never heard of such a thing before and he wanted to consider it more deeply. I AM THE LOVER'S BONES and THE STEP IS DEEP AND HIGH. MATRONEETHA came next and KEEP THOU HOLY THE SABBATH DAY. A shudder came from the engines, that shook the room, as though the Bridge had reversed the screws and they were now to circle around, or go back. The dark girl dropped her pencil and then picked it up again DEATH she wrote and MADNESS and LOVE. THE EMBRACE OF THE SEA AND THE COMMUNION OF WATERS. Sweat shone on her forehead and the page was covered with script and capital letters of all sizes. The ship's doctor twitched the scribbled and written page away to offer a blank sheet THE GLASS COTTAGE and then a drawing of a woman's figure covered with opening windows reaching towards a ship on the sea from a high cliff that was covered with opening windows. Then came a drawing of a black man with an erect penis, his arms in attitude of embracing, and the words IT IS THE SABBATH MY LOVE MY BRIDE. Then the words MAN OVERBOARD and in very small script: *he must have killed himself because he knew we'd get him in New York if not before.* Then the word LOVE written very hard on the white paper with the black pen and finally THE GOLDEN BLOOD MEASURED IN DROPS. The black girl flung the pen so hard against the white metal that it shattered and splashed, then with a grey face fell sideways off her chair. The doctor was at her side immediately, and supported her head as the Professor poured her a glass of water and held it to her lips. His hand jerked and spilled the water on the girl's amethyst dress, she jumped, her eyes came wide open, and when she saw the water on her dress she laughed. 'How was I?' They passed her the sheets, which she perused gravely. 'I remember none of this,' she said, 'just the first doodles, up to these opening boxes.'

* * *

The portable Jung in the ship's library opened at these words 'Psychology teaches us that, in a certain sense, there is nothing in the psyche that is old; nothing that can really, finally die away. Even Paul was left with a thorn in the flesh. Whoever protects himself against what is new and strange and regresses to the past falls into the same neurotic condition as the man who identifies himself with the new and runs away from the past. The only difference is that the one has estranged himself from the past and the other from the future. In principle both are doing the same thing: they are reinforcing their narrow range of consciousness instead of shattering it in the tension of opposites and building up a state of wider and higher consciousness.' The blackboard outside the library that announced the results of the ship's daily lottery, today remarked also that at 11:33 AM by the ship's clocks they would be exactly half way between the old world and the new.

* * *

Three of the passengers would never see America: a murdered girl, a man drowned in the great wake of the vessel, and the murderer of the girl, who would everywhere, always, see only the girl's murder;. and his own action of stuffing her gold watch into the wound was the irrational crown of this act which he would spend the rest of his life expounding in various guises. He was to become a great expert on American affairs. America's beauty moved him to such sobbing, such agonies of grief as if he saw his own girl instead of the landscape, instead of the people. America's exploiters and power-hungry murderers moved him to famished detailed study, social and psychological explorations, in order that he might find justification and explanation for his own act in their rapine, done for gold, thorough and punctual as clockwork. But he never could find justification enough in the deeds of others to assuage his amazement at his own deed. The memory of his murder and the honeyed destructive voluptuousness of it moved his fingers to his penis and to their play upon this sweet instrument of his torture and his vision. Was he the poet, the playwright, the elderly psychologist, the professor, the Indian chief, the actor, for all became experts on America in their own ways, even the one who refused to attain America, and plunged instead into the boiling wake inside her waters, concerning whose act a book was written by a lady who travelled the continent looking at it as though through his eyes?

* * *

She must believe Willa. But it was most important to believe Willa in the right way: not like a parent, or like (whatever the goddess truly was in herself) a disposer of human affairs to whom she, as Willa's priest, was a privileged confidante. She did not believe that the revelation she had had of the *belle indifférence* of Nature and the dead could be wholly false, if it were not entirely as she had been able to see it: she was determined to be a seer with the whole of her capacity, but since she was not the Willa, that capacity was limited, and might very easily falsify at its boundaries with convincing apparitions and images. Thus, *belle indifférence* had for her the pang she was disposed to regard as the note of truth, vibrating deeply and energizing not only joy but sorrow too, and converting the two to what she had labelled for the moment as *la belle indifférence*. She was aware that this was a psychiatric term applied to psychopathic states in which a person could or would not see the consequences of his actions, and was happy in that state; but sometimes she believed that mad people were on the right track. After all, where would she end up if she claimed to others to have talked with the goddess on the high turfs of the Willaparks? There was the other psychiatric term 'signs of reference', which meant that the paranoid schizophrenic believed that events in the world were speaking to him, for his benefit: a swarm of flying ants would announce a girl's period; the sea would murmur in intelligible syllables; a stranger would become the bearer of important messages or qualities, would become London, or Willa, or Harrods for that matter.

It was not, she decided, a one to one, an on and off switching of events she was concerned with: if I do that, such and such a thing will necessarily happen. That would be madness. She believed it was more tidal than that, 'there was a tide in the affairs of men', events flowed, and sometimes they flowed together. The assassination did not cause the great war, nor was the trigger, but rather one of many related events, the greatest visible fact of which was a European war. And in the war, the more a person thought of him or herself as a unique particle the snuffing out of which was an irreplaceable loss, the more paralysed their condition. The great people had understood the flow of events and had made use of them to find the greatest in themselves, and sometimes they embodied the events in opposing powers, as Churchill and Hitler had done. As had all the people who had trained themselves in *la belle indifférence* from concentration camp guards sacrificing millions of lives for the sake of the blood that flowed in their own veins, to keep the race pure; to their white opposite, the doctors and nurses in the hospitals who worked in their healing trades for weeks on end with little or no sleep. Now even the Gods were at threat; the earth goddess was carrying the poisons of industrial waste in her veins, in the seas and rains and rivers; there were weapons available that could split her skin, time-bombs ticking away in deep weapon-silos, (and if the guards of the weapons did not turn their keys in the right switches at the right time, then the attack would launch) and the great garment of ozone that filters the sun's lethal powers from the earth, the garment at which the sun's eyes stop, was eroded and frayed by every kilo of nitric oxide released into the atmosphere by each transatlantic aeroplane flight. Yes she would follow her man to America, in due course, and she would complete the journey when he had not, and she would keep the Glass Cottage, and she would keep faith in the powers that his death had released in her. She grieved in his death, and she rejoiced in it. She had a sudden swift picture of him waving goodbye to her from the side of the great liner, he so high up carried on the black and white mansion that floated, she waving from the customs shed. But now he waved with joy that he was journeying on, and she with joy that she was in the world.

Mankind was at threat, and each person was the half of humanity that was man or the half that was woman. When they met, good or evil could be done on the behalf of the whole of humanity. And the Gods were at threat, for unless they were discerned by man and woman, they became once again mere blind forces working towards man or woman, they became ancestor tree, ancestor stone, ancestor pig; and then tree, stone, pig, moon, sun.

God was not only God, nor human human; both wished to become the other, 'Eternity is in love with the productions of time,' and each in becoming the other became the new thing. This was in her meeting with her Goddess. She thought that her name should now be changed; she would do it by deed poll; she would be by name neither her father nor her dead lover. She would be Willa.

* * *

Budock Combe in New England. That was a strange thing. Budock was such a small village, near Falmouth in Cornwall, hardly more than a church, a few houses, and a farm. The church was very old, rumoured to be more than a thousand years old, the saint that kept his hermitage there had lived before Norman times, and the settlement had taken his name. It seemed strange that somebody from Budock had travelled all this distance and found a new living here, and inspired this neat little village that had been founded when Alexander Pope was writing his Epistles. In the Age of Reason some Cornishman disgusted with the exploitation of his homeland had got out and settled a homestead farm there, and times had been propitious for the little apple-farm, and others had come and bought land and made cider also, and planted more trees on the fertile hillsides and watermeadows. In appearance it was more like Somerset than Cornwall, with its winding streams and rows of willows along the water and along the roads. We drew the car in and asked for a room at the little motel — there was hardly a street, just winding roads with farms, and the motel close to a post office — and we showered and changed our clothes and went out to explore. Attracted by the noise of merrymaking, chanting song, and a fiddle with an accompanying clatter like barrels being beaten with sticks, we came upon this great barn-like habitation against the side of the hill where the road bent round between two large bluffs covered with apple trees scarcely taller than a man but laden with ripe red fruit, so that there seemed more red than green. The farm, or barn, had one of its great dark wooden doors open on a courtyard inside, in which people were dancing on dried grass and on bunches of herbs that gave off an aromatic smell as they were crushed. A tall lean man with steady blue eyes in a brown face, wearing faded overalls, appeared in the doorway, looking at us. He smiled, we smiled, he raised a big china mug in greeting and offered it to us, saying, 'You came to see the apple-combe?' We drank, and said yes, and he took us inside where the dancers circled and the fiddler played and three women beat barrels with wooden staves. An old woman offered us china mugs full of cider, and our guide waited until we had drunk, then eagerly he refilled them. Then we set off down the side of the yard until we came to another large door. The man pulled it aside, and we gasped at the glare of the candles. They were set in tiers around a natural hole in the rock, from which a stream sprung, falling into a great cider barrel, almost as big as a large room. Our guide pointed to the mugs we still carried, and I understood from his gestures that this spring with the barrel cistern, and the system of wooden pipes and a pump, provided all the water used to irrigate the trees, and no other water could be used, as for instance that from streams, as the flavour of the cider and its potency would be affected. With a gesture of great reverence he pointed into the aperture from which the water flowed. The hole was exceedingly mossy, and set in the rock basin was a round green boulder. I looked closer and saw that the very clear water spiralled around this basin and around the boulder that occupied it. The brow was so sloping and the ridges above the eye-sockets were so massive, there was a bony crest on the crown of the skull too, that I did not recognize it for what it was at first, and through what the apple-water flowed. She shrieked and dropped her mug, but the farmer caught it in his great bony hands and the cider he had given us was unspilt.

* * *

A black and white funicular runs on a cable stretched between two mountain villages, one bathed in early sunlight, one still asleep in the shadow of the great peak. A group of people have elected to travel down the mountain at the earliest dawn. As the golden bars of sun shine on the flight-fall of fresh snow, they converge on the cable-car office, muffled in their parkas and gloves and heavy boots, black figures in contrast to the snow, hulking past the pretty fretwork houses still shuttered in the early light. They enter the cable-car, an official of the railway is waiting for them, and touches his glove to the peak of his pill-box hat as they each in turn enter. With a ringing of bells the cable-car disengages itself, and begins its descent of the mountain-side, the ride that in daytime expounds the valleys, but which now is a journey back into the night-time. In the valley-pass, the full moon is still visible, straight in front of them, sinking as they glide on towards her in their air-gondola. Suddenly one of the women is conscious of the humming wire that bears them up, and she looks up at it and its pulley-supports through the glassed roof, as one might look up at a mast or the funnel of a steamship. She is conscious of the music the wire makes as it vibrates between the two villages, the drone of the icy winds across it, the change of its note as the sun heats it and the cold night contracts it, and the note it makes when it is laden with people, and unladen. She remembers in the school-room in the upper village, where she grew up, the master shows how the iron filings arrange themselves on white paper when the magnet is placed below the paper, it is as though they have been waiting for a purpose to follow, and they form a blank bar-space where the magnet's field is too strong for them and they cannot enter it, with two proud bushes of feathery iron spreading from ends, just as the two villages seem to have arranged themselves at either end of the abyssal note sung by the cable-car. Of course the villages were here long before the funicular, but the feeling remains that the mountains in their huge glistening hides came here to listen to the song of the iron that was taken from their sides. People travel great distances to listen to some musician distinguished from among them, and it seems to her that a safe cable-car full of thinking, seeing jellies is a high point of geological evolution, she feels like a specimen being passed for examination in front of the eyes of geology. Something flashes from a distant snow-slope; it is an early skier, perhaps he had his binoculars out and is watching them. She feels that the mountains always intended this cable to be here, to give themselves a good sight of travellers more difficult to inspect when crouched in villages on their flanks, or skiing along their crusty pelts. And they intended this music, this hum, both bass with the length of the cable and seemingly high also with the sense of the minute particles in it, as the mountains are both large and small at once, enormous in their mass, but with a mass made up of infinitely figured individual objects and particles, like snowflakes and granite crystals — God's thoughts. While she felt these things, and felt that the cable stretched between two destinations stood for more than she could see in a short trip between two villages, the men sat together in a huddle. She glimpsed money pass, and a white paper packet; she thought: fools, these criminal actions are likely to get us shot at by rival criminals, why choose this vulnerable and beautiful occasion to trade in heroin.

There was a clang from above. The bracket holding the cable had engaged in its iron slot, and the car was once more rigid at its station. They stepped out on to the concrete platform, and with muttered good-mornings, strode away separately through the snow-lit streets. She walked towards the red glow of the steam locomotive that waited in the small railway station, since her way led down the mountains towards the sea. The furnace door was open, and she could see the driver's silhouette as he bent shovelling coal into the redness. The red eye in the black hulk closed, and the small clang of the closing door came to her clearly across the snow, together with a whiff of the sulphurous coal. She climbed into one of the tall carriages with its buttoned, plush upholstery, and settled down to watch the journey. There were three thousand miles to go towards her new home, and she thought as the sun's gold touched the slopes in front or her, that she was travelling with the sun in the direction of the moon. She did not know which of the two opposite kinds of light she loved most, she loved both of them in their different ways.

* * *

The steel helmet fell into the deep shaft, rebounding from the ladder steps and awakening hoarse echoes that rolled around the hillside like a fountain of noise from the open mine. 'For Christ's sake, Jimmy, why d'dnyou do the strap up? You'll get a sore head walking down there, always assuming nowt falls on it.' There was another helmet in the pack, fortunately, and Jimmy was duly kitted out. He would have had to stay aloft on the hillside, or meet the others down in the valley where the mine adit emerged — nobody could remain unbruised in those corridors where the roof was at times almost too low for a crawl and at others tall as a corridor at Versailles.

They unpacked the rope ladder and threw it over the lip of the square hole in the grass. The little man who had introduced himself as 'the agent' locked again the grilled iron door in the railing that they had passed through. The agent said: 'Remember lads — and lass,' nodding to a helmeted, boiler-suited figure indistinguishable from the others, 'the rope ladder is only a guideline. You should find the main ladder quite whole a few feet down. It will bear your weight — the timber is as sound as when it was set — but it may be slippery. So keep hold of the ladder — you may need it.'

One by one they lowered themselves into the bill's chimney, down into the Devil's Hearth, the infamous mine of Cornwall. It was here, in the deepest levels, that the sea had rushed in and drowned or battered to death sixty-seven miners, in June, 1873, more than a hundred years ago. It was said that at certain hours you could still hear the moans and cries of the drowned millers repeated endlessly over and over, the sounds pouring out of the tunnel and that this was why the mine had been closed. The mine in fact had been closed simply because the price of tin had gone down. You could sometimes hear the mating calls of seals reflected from the cliffs behind on to any part of these hillsides, and at very low tides a syphoning effect of the seawater that still ran in the lower galleries gave rise to a throbbing that could be felt like trains running under the feet, and occasionally heard as a moan and a hiss coming like escaping steam. But the land of Cornwall is haunted by the ghosts of miners, like a kind of thorough and all-pervasive tears that have soaked into these hills, for the land has been ransacked again and again by people interested only in their mineral rights and prices, and not in the faithful, stubborn and deceived people that worked for them, and had so worked back to Phoenician times.

Entering the shaft, their torch beams swung from side to side, plunging into the pit, high into the air above. Jimmy nearly lost his helmet again craning upwards to look at the stars. The shaft was as wide as a small house, and in the torchlight the colour of the rock was blue and green, the variations of amethyst, with slashings of black, and streaks of red from veins of iron that had rusted in the rain. It smelt of ferns and dry rock. They had ventured into the pit on the invitation of 'the agent' who was the legman of a retired professor writing the history of the Cornish mines. Normally it was not easy to visit a closed mine, of which there were so many, and the few remaining working mines were too busy for sight-seers; but it was said of the agent that his master had eyes in every mine in Cornwall, if he so desired. It seemed as dangerous as flying above the ground, to dare the forces of gravity under it.

A great section of ladder, despite the agent's assurances, was missing, and for a space they were obliged to rely on the white nylon ladder, and the friction of their boots on a thirty-degree slope. At length they were at the bottom of the shaft, which was dry and dusty and round as a small ice-rink. With their torches they surveyed the many openings leading off the shaft, including a rounded gap with a parapet in the rock floor that showed where another shaft descended still further. 'We are well below road level now,' said the agent, 'that shaft leads to the sea galleries. Hold the torches still for a moment — I've lost my bearings. Ah there, shine them all together, straight ahead. This is the tunnel.' There was no sign of Jimmy's dropped helmet. They passed through solid amethyst, through dull and hulking scallopings of dark rock, through sheeted billowing blueness stained with the wavy rust of haematite, the blue green aura of copper. They emerged into a great hall lined with other galleries and niches — this was the assembly place for the gangs of miners, each one working independently and paying a percentage for the concession. They passed upwards through the rock, along a narrow corridor cut out of sparkling granite. The agent pointed to recesses at hip level on either side of the tunnel. 'These niches were for the seating-boards. The miner would sit here for a shift of eight hours napping at the solid granite to open the adit up for ventilation and drainage. The dullest, but the safest work.' Crouched and almost bent double the party passed through the work of a man's lifetime measured in feet, a carving of air. There was a sob far back along the tunnel. The agent started, and shone his torch back over the shoulders of the others. Jimmy had taken off his helmet to wipe his face, and had cracked his head painfully against the rock. For a moment prickly hairs had stirred along the backs of everyone there. The agent groped in his pocket and pulled out the key to the padlock that hung from the grille in front of them. In a moment they were all stumbling down a deep grassy slope, and looking up at the stars. The air was cool and fresh; in the mine it had been dusty with their every step, as it had been for the miners who worked there all day and all night. 'Don't you have a wonderful feeling of rebirth?' exclaimed Jimmy. 'I did until you mentioned it,' said the agent, quite out of patience with his party of 'furriners'.

Jimmy had cut his scalp, just a trifling wound on his forehead which had dried in the parched mine, but as he turned out on to the main road back to Truro he wiped his brow with the back of his hand and the cut opened. He looked at his hand and swore, then he felt blood trickling down to the bridge of his nose, it began to run into his right eye. 'This is dangerous,' he thought, and grabbed the steering-wheel as a big car with horn blazing and big eyes bore down upon him and seemed to brush by. The dangerous moment made his bowels churn, they had been uncertain ever since the moment the helmet slipped forwards over his eyes and made him feel he was falling, instead it fell from him straight down the dark hole they had later traversed safely. And that was strange, there had been no sign of it down below. It had, no doubt, bounced and rolled straight into the gallery that led to the forbidden sea-passages. Now the blood veil falling forward over his eyes was reminding him of this and causing a new vertigo, he must stop the car and get out.

He did so, and was seized with a completely irresistible desire to defecate. Wildly, he looked round him, there was no toilet, no paper, no seclusion, just the grass verge by a main road at a little past midnight. He dropped his trousers, alert and anxious for new headlights along the road: the night felt cool and still, and his own car's side lights made little difference to the darkness. As he uncovered his behind, the night seemed to him to become cooler and sweeter, and his anxiety about being overlooked, or caught by some police patrol, almost disappeared. He tucked his trousers and underpants well forward round his ankles, and squatted as far down as he could — in good time, for as he lowered himself, his shit leapt out with a warm and complete feeling. He heard it splash in the grass a surprising distance behind him, with a liquid spatter. A feeling of enjoyment in this act was new to him, he felt the grass and smelt the damp manury warmness of the night, and then realized that it was partly the smell of himself that he was enjoying. The exploration through the mine came back to him, not the rigid and awkward thing that it had been at the time, and he the butt of the party, being used by the experienced little agent as the 'awkward' squad to ease the tension of danger, the butt and scapegoat who made everyone else graceful and skilful by comparison (and he himself as privileged fool under the special care of the agent, so he also came to no harm). Now it was taking its place in his memory as a voyage through the rooms of the green-clothed hill of serpentine and amethyst, in the anterooms of the secret and lethal chambers of the sea, where strange polyps felt through the bones of drowned miners, and where he, Jimmy, was neither alive or dead, but a spirit exploring nature with a light lashed to his wrist by a lanyard. It was a good name, he thought, for the tunnels of the mine: 'gallery'. He remembered now with perfect recall for a few blissful minutes the great abstract pictures the rocks and minerals had made fused together under the action of water, and how the contoured painting of the tunnel showed by their sections, the contours of the whole hill — solid stone though it was, he could see by the variations and stresses of the stone — wall-paintings, the nature of that hill; as though his eyesight had dissolved in it like living rain or miners' tears.

* * *

He went every month to the black man at the radio station office, who gave him a cheque for $140. This covered the rent on his flat, and had done so for nearly eighteen months. They had been introduced to each other at a college party; it was the chairman of the department's birthday. The martinis were very strong, and pot was being smoked in the back room. A very good joint had been made for him back there, he smoked it with immense pleasure, for often his lungs had been troubled by the harshness of the cut weed.

Intense relaxation permeated his body, and he became absorbed in the intricate details of an oil painting hanging opposite him. It was a scene of people talking and drinking in a room, done in a thick impasto, with layers of black, blue, and gold paint. The voices in the room in which he sat now appeared to come from the figures in the painting, and every now and again one of these painted figures moved his head to glance over his shoulder at the watcher, as a shadow or light fell on the canvas and altered the texture of the paint, or another of the painted figures would put the canape he was holding to his mouth; there were two women painted close together and he saw that they quickly kissed and looked out at him, pleased and guilty.

Occasionally one of the flesh-and-blood guests stood in front of the picture for a while, and then he would seem to be conversing with the painted members of the party with his back to the room or he might disappear, as the texture of his hair and clothes merged with the thick built-up paint. The watcher felt a strong hand on his shoulder. He turned and looked into an immense black face that was crying, tears made the cheeks shine like patent leather. 'Are you lonely?' said the watcher to the black face. It nodded and laid itself heavily on his shoulder.

It was late. The host and hostess were handing around cups of coffee which, offered late, were an infallible sign of a desired departure in that part of America. The watcher looked around for the black face, but all the faces were caucasian. He wondered whether that excellent pot had given him an outright hallucination.

The following week he received through the mail a letter with the heading of the local radio station WC32 1NW. On it there was a sketch in coloured crayon of a black head lying on a white shoulder, and the figures 6:30 PM underlined many times in black. He drove to the radio station not knowing what to expect. A silent janitor let him in and pointed down a rubberized corridor with a notice that said 'disc studio'. The same notice on a pair of swinging doors led him into a large room with a glass panel let into the further wall. There was a great deal of radio apparatus standing around, and a sharp smell of electricity like fresh weather in the air. Behind the glass panel like a lone fish in an aquarium the black man paced about and gesticulated into a row of microphones, switched on a gramophone turntable with a quick gesture, and sat down on a bent-steel chair. He was in his shirt-sleeves and even from across the room the sweat shone on his face.

When the black man saw that his visitor had arrived he made signs through the glass for him to sit down in front of the glass panel and relax. Meanwhile, the record had ended and the black man began his silent spiel once more, that flowed silently and insensibly but for the fresh smell of electricity, through the room, silently through the head of the visitor, through the buildings, and out through the streets until it met a radio set tuned to its own vibration, which it would also pass through, turning some of its energy to the squawking vital tones of the city's best salesman and commercial disc-jockey speaking and selling to three million people on WC32 1NW.

In the radio station control room, there was no noise. The visitor took out his smokes and rolled a cigarette: it was the excellent grass he saved for the winter, when his lungs felt weak. With its aid he contemplated the black man in his window, in his frame hanging on the wall, as he would any other work of visual art, in complete silence. At twelve-thirty the frame became vacant. The visitor expected the disc-jockey to come out into the room on his side of the glass and talk to him, but nobody arrived; he realized that if the black man did come it would break the silence, and that would be inappropriate. Suddenly many of the lights went off, leaving only a glow from the radio apparatus, and a small light from a bracket on the wall. It was time to leave. He walked out of the front of the building, and the glass doors closed after him with a snick as the automatic bolt closed.

A week later the first cheque for $140 arrived. Since then he had responded to the summons and received his cheque eighteen times. He had been worried in case his accountant had queried the cheques, for although he had done nothing wrong, he would not care to explain his relationship with the black man. But the accountant put them down as 'fee for freelance services' without a murmur.

* * *

The apples of America have made a better adjustment to insects than have the apples of England. When I first saw the apple-trees with the fruit constellated in their boughs and many individual fruit lying underfoot in the shade, I warned her. I had heard that the wasps and yellow-jackets and hornets of America and such varmints were dangerous creatures, and that in the summer people carried syringes of adrenalin, the only effective first aid. With the fruit lying under the tree where it could be rolled by a careless foot, one of these monsters might very well fly out of his cavernous undercutting, out of his cider-delving, to sting badly the foot or leg of either one of us. So I warned her. But she bent down and picked up one of the large yellow fruit, just such a ripe fruit lying that I would have imagined might contain the worst of insects in twos and threes, angry at their apple-comfort disturbed. But the skin was unmarked and unbreached. She took a bite and handed it to me, the juice fizzed through my gums, it was warm and spiritous, like the bouquet of a brandy, from the sun. I looked up into the thickly pleached branches. They were set as thick with leaves as a lichen is with its fronds, and in the green, yellow apples glowed and rolled. We gathered a few, she bit into one that I could see had a large smear of chalky bird-shit on it. I took this from her and handed her my own.

The skins must be marginally thicker than the mandibles of the insects are strong. The apples have kept one step ahead of the insects. The crops are sprayed too, which makes them dangerous unwashed for humans; I believe that the apples protect themselves against these dangerous poisons by growing thicker skins, which protect them against the insects, even though the latter have developed resistances against the crop sprays. So the spray defeats the insects still. Thus the apple-harvest is closer with its warm sparkling blood to us than either of us are to cold and jointed insects. It refuses its benefits to insects, bestows them on us. It is for this life-sparkle that the insects seek out the apples, to drink their nectar and to line nests with apple-pulp and skin. But what is a coconut but an apple that resists the teeth? We take our apples home from the supermarket and soon finish them, but thirst for more. There are red apples in the great white refrigerator, though these red apples have tougher skins, and their juice does not sparkle as fondly as the fresh-picked sun-warmed apples. But when you pierce the leathern bottle of their skin and drink the cool juice you are in a kind of heaven. I took a great snap out of my apple to see the star inside. I made a fantasy of Jesus as the second Adam, meeting a second Eve.

Eat the apple this way, she said to Jesus,
Stretching legs and arms wide like a
Five-pointed star; like this? asked Jesus,
Stretching arms and legs wide making a
Six-pointed star; no, she said, like this,
Presenting him his apple with the dusty calyx
Raised to his lips, she gripping
The stem in thumb and finger.
                                        Jesus took
A large red bite which blazed white
Across the fruit, and with the bright
Juices fizzing in the sweet flesh
And in his teeth where Jesus' juices
Rose to those juices, He saw where He had severed
A star like a five-pointed woman who had
Folded herself out of the ground,
And out of the air, deep
Through the tree's wood,
And expressed herself in every orchard fruit,
Star deep in every applewood staff
Beyond the wood-grain: in those starry depths
Persephone wrapped in cool appleskin.

It was a great amenity to have in the flat a refrigerator large enough to store our fruit so that it came out chilled like iced drinks. Besides apples and ordinary oranges there were nectarines and peaches and a fruit called tangerinos, which despite their name were closer to a small sweet grapefruit than to either an orange or a tangerine. Would the insects ally themselves with the husked fruit to produce the dangerous wasp-o-nut that taken out of the large white refrigerator (which with its light on looked as roomy as a ship's cabin), would stir under your fingers, sting you and eat you until you got a thicker skin. In England we were not afraid of the wasps, they were domesticated, and we dressed our footballers in jerseys that resembled them, unlike the jointed helmeted and padded footballers of America who resembled robotic machines rather than sportsmen. Indeed, it was due to a wasp sting that I conceived my first son:

A wasp hanging among the rose-bines:
Footballer wandering in an antique market.

Again he struck the wasp with the sheets of paper and
Believes he kills it; the wasp
Clinging to the tendon of his ankle looked very
 sporting and official
In black and gold clinging by the tail the high
 pitched pain
Was yellow streaked with black oaths

He could not find the wasp-body it had been sucked
Along his nerves. After the rage
There is a sore pain turning to lust

That afternoon a plucky infant was conceived
Full of an infant's rage and juices
He struck once and conceived

He struck as the wasp once, his child
Ran in out of the garden, bawling like a plucky infant
Teased among gigantic cousins in a striped football jersey
 beyond endurance.

Indeed, it is the custom to sit among the insects in a hot English summer garden, suffering the small bites, drowsing happily to the drone of insects plying from bush to bush over the level green lawns, 'Well played Sir', and a spattering of applause from the somnolent spectators to the click of red leather against white willow among the thin white cricketers in their pattern like fallen stars on the green grass. Sometimes a man might rise to the irritation of a wasp, and gallantly bat it away as the famous cricketer easily and with grace bats away the humming red ball; but in America they sell small chemical warfare devices, the fuse of which you light, and retire immediately, that give off a pervasive crystalline smoke settling without trace, which is guaranteed to repel all insects from the garden during a certain time, kill those already present, and poison your guests if they are not careful about what they touch while they are eating.

But in England you do not have a hornet that will fell a horse in its field, nor mosquitoes that carry encephalitis that after a fever of horrors will leave a child an idiot, and unable to conceive in mind or body ever again.

* * *

One of the things that irritated him about America was the immense silliness of the furniture. The enormous stream-lined refrigerator looking like a hygienic safe-vault, the tremendous wasteful electric cookers whose ovens got so hot that you could boil saucepans on top without turning on the rings; the silly big colour television sets fitted into phoney antique cabinets and sideboards, so whelked and beaded with ornamentations, fruits and vines that they resembled a Cruikshank drawing of the old curiosity shop, or the storytelling machine, some drawing-room secretary of sorting and memory-drawers, and not the modern invention for keeping whole families in a hypnotic sleep for several hours each day. He was sure the euphemistic carpentry in this last case was a deliberate softening of the nature of the instrument. It would be different if the little drawers opened, to hold story-books or buttons or slippers. But they were a facade, and the whole frontage was a veneer to the alien scribbled television interior, the shockingly surgical vehicle of the saccharine and bloody stories the instrument combed out of the air with its aerials on every house, resembling gigantic astrological signs.

There was very much of this facade idea in the ordinary houses. Built for the main part of the most up-to-date insulating materials arranged to enclose box-like interiors, once the utilitarian purpose had been served of enclosing a territory in tough and drab matchboarding, plastic and asbestos sheeting, and a coat of neutral colour applied, the euphemistic fripperies began. Plasticwooden colonial sideboards and whatnots in imitation walnut, beds with pillars and knobs and hangings, foolish little magazine racks with fringes, stools and rocking chairs of moulded wood, pirated William Morris curtains (called 'drapes' and drawn in the antique fashion with cords and pulleys), nylon candlewick bedspreads, anything and everything to conceal the cheap utility of the building with vulgar excursions into a plastic past. No doubt there were many quotations from famous styles and pieces, but the general effect was cluttered, dark, dusty, and at least fifty years old.

He was of that opinion until one bathtime. He was utilitarian about his baths — they prevented insomnia and kept him clean, that was all. So he took them late at night. On this occasion he had been working hard at his desk and was lifting his sixth cup of strong coffee to his lips when his hand gave a nervous jerk and poured, seemingly quite slowly, the lukewarm coffee in a spreading stain like a freckle of old age all over his white shirt-front and black-and-white striped linen trousers. He looked down astonished at himself, at the spreading stain, and at the clinging shirt. Unexpectedly his tits glowed at his next thought, which was that he would get straight in the bath with all his clothes on, to wash the coffee out before it stained. He got into the tub and turned the shower on. The warm water clung to his clothed skin like a great caress, as though he were lightly caught in some god's immense palm, and held, balanced, in the rain and the open air. The light friendly grip of his wet clothes, and the shine on him as the water fell down made him masturbate. Afterwards he felt clean and empty and pleasantly tired. He stripped the clothes off and dropped them in the hand basin. He sat in the warm and soapy water recalling the voyage in the great liner, and how the dead woman's photograph was tacked on the public board (all the passengers were photographed, ostensibly so that they would buy the expensive prints, but perhaps for security too. The photographer caught all embarking passengers by surprise in a festive little anteroom at the top of the gangway.) Her photograph stayed there looking pleased throughout the voyage, even after her murder, and people pointed it out together, secretly, confidingly, pleased to be in the secret that was by the time they docked, no secret. It was strange seeing that one dead woman among all the living, no different-looking from all the others, a photograph like the rest of them, but behind her photograph was dead, clean flesh that would never dirty on its own account, that would never sweat, clean and unsweating in its white refrigerator, the black hair in the dark beyond the cold-seal, clean and cold with waxy static blood, protected from all change until the processes of the cremation or the burial were initiated. Just as we conjecture about the photograph of a celebrity, so this woman's expression appeared wiser and more contained in the photograph than those of the other passengers, and so very much more inaccessible.

As he stood up to dry himself, he noticed for the first time a design frosted on the top margin of the bathroom mirror. It had escaped his eye until now, no doubt because his eye had dismissed it along with all the other irrelevant ornamentation in the flat, designed to comfort people with a background and troubles different from his own, English ones. This design cut into the glass, bevelled and frosted, no doubt by some machine and not a living craftsman, was of a spray of lily-of-the-valley that crossed a fleur-de-lys design with triple leaves caught up in the centre by a flowing ribbon into a bundle, and cut across with a retaining crescent shape that cupped the upper part of the triple lys-fronds. Eclectic, ham-fisted, repetitious as his usual mood would have found this design, had it been noticed at all, now the crescent shone white in the steamed-up mirror, bevelled away to the light, with a purity like the settling steam, simple, and automatic because instinctive, like the rising moon. The design became a small white figure dancing through the steamy glass, the crescent its upward-spread arms. Startled with this pleasure, he dried himself and walked into the living-room. The colour television story-telling machine was no longer a commercial effrontery, but a riot of humorous and affectionate invention, the rocking chair had shed its origins in the plastic factory and was a local character, traditional, accepted, a person who belonged on the stoop as a reminder to the street that the family face endured and sons knew sons as grandfathers knew grandfathers. Out of the window, the great anchor-shaped patch of trees that he had feared to walk in because he had once seen a big snake sneak in off the road, beckoned to him with ancient feelings of red indians and resinous camp-fires. He finished drying himself, and got into rough trousers and stout boots. He thought he could learn a great deal now about the place he was living in if he walked among the trees until the sun came up.

* * *

When the Professor wanted to know what was 'in the wind', what people really thought without knowing that they thought it, what the local *Zeitgeist* said, he persuaded his students to do a special exercise. The exercise was to write, for twenty minutes or so every day, at a conveniently receptive or relaxed time, just whatever came into one's head. You were not to worry about phrasing or meaning, or even handwriting, but you were to present to the Professor, in a fortnight's time, a script of 'automatic writing' done by you, but without your knowledge, since it was a strict rule that the putative author of each script was by no means even to glance at his own script until the Professor himself had seen it. The Professor claimed to be able to look into the student's future by this means, to decipher in the garbled paragraphs those nuts or buds of meaning that were, once noted, to unfold in the student's life and work and in his attitudes also to his teachers and career. Sometimes — almost always — the Professor knew that the sulphurous fumes of scribbled irritation and anguish would clear to reveal a farmstead, perhaps, with a slinky pigpen of silky mud; a favourite toy long forgotten; a secret garden illuminated with fairy lights that trembled in the little fountain at the centre; a black man gesticulating silently behind a window; a vast empty ocean liner carrying no passengers, no crew, only the white corpse of a murdered woman; a littoral full of expectation and the heave of the shingle in the heavy waves. When the scripts cleared in this manner the Professor felt he could advise the student to settle his mind at any time that he needed by entering this place and doing whatever took his fancy to do, or entering this spot and waiting for some phantasm to arrive and whisper to him — softly some truth that proved that such phantasms were not fancies. Time and time again he had been able to direct a student to that part of his mind where conflicts disappeared and territories met, where personages unacknowledged by the conscious ego of the student held significant deliberations — perhaps with the intention of being overheard, since every student who had attended to the unfolding of this entered fantasy gained intelligence and vitality, and began in his youth to teach his teacher.

In fact, the Professor took the *sortes* from the young people, he took the oracle of his students, and the oracle has usually spoken to most effect when it has been listened to seriously. Now he had begun to do this. He had suffered from many visitations of the white ship, white now with the whiteness of cold fat, through which pumped blood and brine by means of the round sliced holes of the ports. This ship that was a bleeding section of some greater anatomy had drawn up outside his bedroom window; he had heard jazz and thinking it was some late nightcomers from a fraternity house rose from bed ready to reason them away from his window, but as he clutched the cords that pulled the drapes apart the music went ghostly and he saw through the parting curtains the great cliff of white fat through which salt and bloody music pumped as though sliced arteries. He had woken lying on the floor of his bedroom under the window. The drapes were closed, but in his mind he could still hear and see the music pumping with the gore and hear people calling from the decks 'he's awake, he's awake!' He wondered if this were an experience of the collective unconscious announcing some visitor from the deeps, some constellation for good or evil in the outer world, or whether it was a private disorder, as he suspected. So he called the *sortes* from younger heads than his own.

And full of grievance they were too. The usual moaning about the system's corruption in which personal grievance was indistinguishable from ingrowing idealism in a situation endlessly cushioned by suave executive professors and academic administrators. He was surprised and touched to find that he appeared in thin disguise in three of the scripts — he was convinced the students concerned were unconscious of the compliment — as a listener and a watcher on the bridge of a great ocean-going vessel plying between the old world and the new. In the one the figure was developed by showing the ship as a kind of fruit that sucked nutriment of passengers at one shore, matured them during the week's voyage by good food and entertainment into fertile seeds, and then let them out on the opposite shore to mingle with the good soil of their antithetical world and germinate plentifully. This notion of the ship censing like a poppy seed-case from side to side its useful and thriving passengers, with himself an executive sprite of the service — growing old in his seedmanship and unable to remain at rest on land, like the Flying Dutchman — tickled the Professor's depressed self-esteem so hard that he laughed aloud to conceal the small snuffiness of emotion which he then hid away in his hankie.

It was hardly surprising that the ship came into their automatic scripts. He had mentioned it several times in conversation, and once to introduce his inaugural lecture. He knew that he arrived charged with the energy of a visitor from a foreign and quaint place, where people spoke with chopped voices and never drawled, that was eternally covered with Holmesian peasoup fog. He had special mana for a few days at least, and he took the opportunity to reinforce the image of the worn and experienced traveller by describing a few details of his journey, though he could not bear to mention the murder.

The last student of the forty *sortes* he examined was a dark, quiet girl, who he at first suspected of having no unconscious whatsoever. He gave her a cup of coffee from the departmental coffee-urn and a book of his own to glance at, then started to read. Exaltation; depression; laziness; hyper-activity; the usual thing, but here, a difference — at the end of each section where her casual mind described ineptly some doing of the day as boring, or exciting, black or white, there came a sentence of chilling precision that named one or the other tinge. Finally, two sentences of this kind abutted directly upon each other: My fingernails black as mica in the flint; my feelings like moonlight scribbling on the lake. The moods of opposition vanished, and one of the clear spaces he always looked for became visible: 'they whipped the top and the top saw images. It was a hollow mountain and there was a white tissue that was salty whipping it from below. The top grew clouds for a hat and it grew birch on its slopes. Deer started running upon the top, helping it to spin, and it spun with a high note and a deep note. A man stepped from the top with a questioning look, and stepped back on the mountain slopes. Rain sprang from the whirling clouds and the rainbows were all twisted and coiled by the humming of the top so it seemed the rainbows danced while the rain fell and the sun shone and hummed in spirals up the hill and they are trampling the young woman into the ground. Ah what a cruel death by stamping into the ground but the rainbows hum and the deer run and the men and the women feed well on yams through the winter . . .' 'Well,' he said, quite roughly, 'you have been paying a lot of attention to your anthropology professors!' 'What?' 'I say you have been soaked through and through in anthropologist's juice. You are taking an anthropology course?' 'Yes, I am.' 'Well,' he said, really very crossly, 'I didn't want you to reproduce, merely reproduce the substance of other lectures just to please me, you see, I wanted your mind to play with itself and me and not with other professors.' The girl blushed. 'I'm sorry, Professor. What is it that offends you?' Her voice had a midstate twang, not a drawl, very precise with the margins of each word, which she formed carefully in her mouth as if each were some small transparent sculpture that nevertheless had significant weight. 'The story of Hainuwele.' 'Hainuwele, Professor. I'm afraid I don't know . . .' 'They must have told you . . .' Then he remembered with a chill the book he had put by mistake in his bag this morning. It was one he had not needed, and when he groped in his big briefcase for his lecture-books, he was at a loss to know how it could have got there. It contained the story of Hainuwele. 'Look, look at this in your script. Do you remember it?' 'No, Professor, not at all. I like it too, I don't often like what I write. 'Now look at this here, the story of Hainuwele . . .'

* * *

HAINUWELE climbed into the coconut, says. Climbed into the coconut before the world was, says. Coconut swam always in the sea, says. Man's dog smelt a wild pig, says. Pig took flight in water, says. Pig drowned in the water, says. Man found coconut on tusk of wild pig, says.

Man planted coconut in his yard, says. In three days the palm was tall, says. In three more days the palm full of blossom, says. Man climbed palm for blossom, cut finger, says. Blood fell on leaf, says. Where blood fell face of maiden, says. Three days later, trunk of maiden, says. Three days later, little girl grown, says. Three days later full grown woman, says.

HAINUWELE not like ordinary person, says. HAINUWELE's shit full of good things, says. Father grew rich, says. Chinese gongs, mirrors, lovely dresses in shit of maiden, says. Time for the Nine Dance, says. HAINUWELE in centre of dance, says. Rich maiden passing betel nut to men, says. Men dancing nine-fold snake, says.

SECOND NIGHT HAINUWELE gave them coral instead, says. They liked coral, dancers, women, children wanted more coral, says. THIRD NIGHT HAINUWELE gave them thin white dishes, says. FOURTH NIGHT HAINUWELE gave big white dishes, says. FIFTH NIGHT HAINUWELE gave bush knives, says. SIXTH NIGHT HAINUWELE gave betel boxes, says. SEVENTH NIGHT HAINUWELE gave golden earrings, says. EIGHTH NIGHT HAINUWELE gave glorious gongs, says.

NINTH NIGHT men dug deep pit, says.

HAINUWELE in centre to pass out gifts, says. LESIELA men pressed her into the pit, says. The great song drowned out her cries, says. They trampled her into the earth, says.

FATHER pokes stick into the dancing ground, says. Stick covered with blood and hairs, says. Father digs, cuts HAINUWELE into pieces, says. The pieces grow into food, says. Her sister curses the people, says. Holding the two arms of HAINUWELE she curses them, says. Sister builds a ninefold spiral gate, says. Tells people to come through gate to her, says.

SOME PEOPLE got through the gate, says. Some people failed to pass gate, says. People who reach the sister of HAINUWELE are people, says. People who fail become certain animals, says. People who fail become certain spirits, says. Only when you die will you see me again, HAINUWELE says.

* * *

I want you to understand, said the poet, that we are ruled by the moon. I don't mean poets, I mean all men. Women are ruled by themselves, by the moon-nature in them; that is, they are not ruled by the moon: they are the moon. It is in this manner that they are our door to the universe: the moon walks about on the surface of this planet. And the moon, as womankind and its own self, is the Grail. This is the meaning of the saying, the World is in the Grail and the Grail is in the World, since the World is within the spiral tidal influence of the Moon, and womankind also ruled by this influence, walks and talks and makes love and discovers and rules on the surface of the World.

So far, I am saying no more than what you may dismiss as simple poeticizing. What is this talk of Grails and Moon-goddesses, you may say, turn it into poems, lad, and be respected. Very well, then, I will tell you what you do not wish to know, in case you find that woman is a goddess, and that you are her consort and must perform the responsibilities of a consort, or lose the World. You have forgotten if you ever knew that the flowers of human reason and ability have roots, and these flowers spring from what roots are compelled to burrow and feed in, the soil, the disjecta, the despised of the world.

If a man resists his destiny, even if he is only a child, then we know he falls ill. The illness may be a first warning, and in that illness he may have dreams or visions which give him information concerning that destiny. He may still ignore these, being told by his doctors or parents or companions that such visions and dreams are more epiphenomena of his illness, merely phantasms. Then in due course he will become well, and the visions will have gone, and something in him that was alive will have left also, for the reason that he did not heed the voices in him. If a man resists his destiny, even if he is only a child, then he will fall ill.

Will you now tell me what time in his life a man has the greatest chance of falling ill? (Voices from the audience: *After potato chips and beer with the late late horror show* (Jeers). *At puberty. When he is in love. After divorce or separation.*)

You are quite right of course, all of these affect one's

sensitivity to the inner voices and the outer infection (which may also be a voice) even the potato chips and beer, for beer is a little wicket gate into the unknown, just as puberty is. But you have the incorrect emphasis. The statistics show (the lights dim and an immense graph appears on the screen behind the lecturer's head) that a man has an increased chance of illness in particular once a month. That often. Or a chance of initiatory dreams, of ideas, of deep-drawing instinctive love, or whatever way his destiny takes him. And here is the other half of the graph, superimposed on the last. Because woman has also an inevitable chance of being sick, or if she accepts *her* destiny, her visions, understanding of herself, if she understands and watches her bodily changes, an inevitable chance of being exceptionally well, exactly once a month. (Gasps from audience.)

* * *

Gretel was just ten. Her mother had altered so much recently. Disagreement with the pots and pans in the kitchen at every mealtime, scalding liquids splashed, plumes of smoke and the clashing of saucepan lids: Gretel no longer enjoyed making a doll house out of the kitchen table when mother was cooking. Gone were the days when Gretel could go anywhere she pleased — her mother had actually boxed her ears when she found the little girl trying on one of her skirts. It was as though another mother had arrived in the house, and her voice had acquired a punch and a timbre to it that made little Gretel's head ache.

One day Gretel's little brother, Hansel, took her by the hand. 'Our mother has changed so,' he said, 'that life in her house no longer seems worth living. She cooks our food, yes, but with such cursings and swearings that it is difficult to swallow. If we go near her when she is in a calmer mood, she pushes us away, saying she is too busy. The little dog is in a better position than we are, since when she swears at him, he bares his teeth and snarls back, and this amuses her, and she gives it some food. Gretel,' he said, 'let us travel over the world and find a better household and a better mother.'

So they walked all day long over the meadows and they came

to a forest. At the edge of the forest they found a great tree to sleep in, all soft and odorous inside, and they wished that this was their home, so they crawled inside and slept soundly.

In the morning, the sun was shining and the tree felt safe and strong, but Gretel's head ached and Hansel complained how thirsty he was. They took each other by the hand and went in search of a brook until they saw the water-light reflecting through the trees, smelt water in the air and heard the whispering gurgle of the running water. Hansel lay on the mossy bank, stretched out, and dipped his hand in the water to drink — but suddenly Gretel stopped him. 'Sister, what is the matter, I am so thirsty!' 'I heard the stream speaking to me. It whispered: "Whoever drinks me will turn into a tiger." Brother, I am so afraid that you will be turned into a tiger and make me bleed with your great claws, and tear me in pieces in this beautiful place.' 'Very well, Gretel,' replied her brother, 'we will drink from another stream.'

They came to another stream, and Hansel bent to drink, but his sister cried out, 'Ah Hansel, do not drink here, you will be turned into a wild wolf and tear me to pieces. I heard the stream whispering "Whoever drinks me now will be turned into a fierce wolf who will eat his sister." Sister, I am so parched. Come what may, I will drink at the next stream.' So they travelled on, and when they came to the next stream, it spoke to Gretel: 'Whoever drinks here will become a fawn,' so she said to her brother, 'Dear Brother, do not drink here either, for you will be turned into a fawn, and run away from me.' 'Nevertheless,' replied Hansel, 'I must drink from this stream, for it is time for me to quench my thirst.' So he crouched on the bank and put his lips to the water, and as soon as he did so his clothes became a velvet skin, and his hair dwindled until it became velvet, and his eyes grew large and dark, and he turned into a fawn.

Gretel wept sadly over the poor creature by the stream bank, and the fawn looked sadly back at her. 'Don't fret, poor beautiful creature. I will always stay with you and take care of you and we will find a place where we can live together.' She took off the golden necklace she wore and put it round the fawn's neck, and she made a soft cord of rushes to lead it. Further into the peaceful wood they went, and after they had travelled most of the day, they came to a little abandoned woodman's cottage.

So Gretel took some twigs, and fastened them to a branch, and swept out the cottage. She gathered moss and leaves and made a soft bed for them both; and in the fresh morning sunlight she gathered nuts and berries for herself to eat, and young grass for the fawn, who ate out of her hand, and played and frisked with her, and made her very happy. 'If only poor Hansel could turn into his proper self, how happy we should be,' she thought.

It happened that the king of the country in which the forest grew and in which Hansel and Gretel lived their lives was fond of hunting deer in company with his court, and with dogs, and that he held his hunt on this occasion near to the little woodman's cottage. When the fawn heard the dogs baying and the horse neighing, the hunting horns and the shouts of men, he lifted his head and sniffed the air, and said, 'Dear Sister, the hunt is very sweet to me, I must go out and be hunted, and try my wits against the pack.' Gretel was horrified that he should wish to risk all that they had together, but he pleaded so long and so hard that at last she agreed that he should join the hunt. 'But promise me that you will return in the evening,' she said, 'tap on the door and say, Sister, Sister, let me in, and you will be safe again. But be sure to use these words, otherwise I will not know who it is, and I will not open the door.' So the fawn sprang out of the cottage and into the woods, and before long the huntsmen caught sight of it, and blew their little horns, and galloped after it, but however hard they tried they could not keep up with the fawn, who leapt into a thicket and was gone just as the sun set. So the king gave up the hunt for that day, though he was determined to try for the fawn the next day, and the little animal crept home in the darkness and tapped on the door of the cottage and said, 'Sister, Sister, let me in,' which she did.

The next morning they were woken by the sounds of the hunt, and the fawn lifted his head, and his nostrils flared and he said, 'Sister, I must go out and join the hunt again, for the sun is high in the sky, and the dogs are barking and I can smell the resin of excitement in the air.' So his sister let him out, reminding him that he must say when he tapped at the door, 'Sister, Sister, let me in.' Once again, when the king and his huntsmen caught sight of the fawn with the golden collar they gave chase, and they hunted all day, but the little fawn was too quick and clever for them. Not quite clever enough, however, because at one point he was nearly surrounded, and one woodsman wounded him in the foot before he could take his great leap into the thicket behind which the little cottage stood, and he jumped lamely and the woodsman was able to follow him home. The man crouched by the door as the little fawn tapped on the door and said, 'Sister, Sister let me in,' and as the door closed he wheeled and ran back to the king, to tell him all that had happened. The king said only, 'Then tomorrow we shall have another chase.'

Gretel was terrified to see that the fawn had begun to bleed. She washed the little wound, and applied healing herbs, and told the fawn that it must go to bed now, and rest, and in the morning it would be well again. To be sure, in the morning no trace of the wound was to be seen, it was so small; but when the horns blew and the dogs began to bay, the little fawn said, undeterred by his experience, 'Dear Sister, let me go out into the sunshine and the chase. If I do not I shall die here. But when I hear the horns blow I feel like an animal that could fly!' So Gretel had to let the little fawn out of the cottage once again.

All day she waited, lonely and frightened in the little cottage they had shared so happily. Now, she believed, he had gone out in the wood to his death, perhaps even now he had been pulled down, and the huntsmen were sharing his poor body among the hounds, huntsmen splashed with blood and with red knives and darkened arms. The sun had set, and it was quite dark when a soft tapping came at the door and a whisper, 'Sister, Sister, let me in,' and with great joy she got off the bed where she had been lying and went to the door and opened it. A tall man stood there, with a golden crown; it was not her fawn who had returned but a crowned king! Gretel was so frightened at this, but very fascinated, and became less frightened when the king took her by the hand and spoke kindly to her. 'Will you come with me to my palace and be my wife?' he said. When the door opened he did not know what to expect, some woodland ogre or witch perhaps, and he kept his hand firmly on his sword. But there stood one of the most beautiful maidens he had ever seen, and his heart went out to her at that moment. 'I will come with you,' replied the maiden, 'but if you have killed my fawn, I will kill you in your bed.' But then the little fawn with the golden collar sprang over the threshold, and they all stood together in great happiness in Gretel's woodland cottage, and the woodsman slammed down on the table a great bloodstained pouch containing the carcass of the deer that they had caught in the wood, together with two rabbits, and they all laughed happily, thinking of the great banquet that was to come, for it was a long time since Gretel had had a piece of meat to eat.

* * *

The wild hunt, said the poet, and the shedding of blood: in this drama there are at least three personages: a king and a queen and a beast, and there are many transformations which vary according to the times we live in. There may be a king and a queen and the beast is an anthill, or a termitary; or the king may dissolve into the Houses of Parliament; the queen seeks her daughter or the daughter seeks her mother, and this is like the quest of Demeter for Persephone. The king may be the beast, until the queen releases him with a loving kiss; or the king may release the queen (who may begin as a commoner or a princess before she becomes queen) by cutting through a dense and tangled wood inhabited by beasts. But whatever else, all the tales, told at the mother's or nurse's laps, speak to the child of what is coming to her, or coming to him through her; the changes and the shedding of blood. If the boy grows up refusing this knowledge and refusing women, there will still be changes and shedding of blood, for that is inevitable, but the change will be an icy one, and the blood will be shed by men in battle, and the less that is listened to, the greater will be the war. One day these changes will be known and followed by man and woman alike, who will be agile in their transformations and, as the Apocryphal gospel says, 'The garments of shame will be trampled underfoot, and the male will become as the female, and the female the male.'

Thank you for your patience in listening to me — there is no way in which this theme can be told — except in stories, parables;

but perhaps my discourse will enable you — and I, ashamed by my inability to tell of such matters in academic terms, I shall try harder to live them — will enable you to see the importance of the tales, and how they have always been clamouring to help us in our daily life.

With that, the poet sat down. For a moment, there was silence. Then the gallery, largely filled with the women students' caucus, began to applaud. The front rows of professors, assistant professors, and associate professors craned to see who was applauding, but then the Chairman of English, who happened to be a lady, and also the immediate sponsor of the poet's visit, began to clap, and the whole hall followed suit. 'Our visitor will be happy to answer questions . . .' began the chairman as the applause died down, but the poet blushed and waved the questions away, crossed to where his girl friend was sitting, and took her hand.

However, that night the poet's dreams were full of madwomen and blood, and bacchantes gralloching poets who had run naked through the trees. He was caught, and felt the black-bladed knife press on his skin, and gave himself up for lost — but as soon as he had done so he was taken through the wood to a great throne made of white wood that turned slowly, and on that throne were three queens, and the throne was carved very curiously with fruiting vines, and apple trees, and beast faces that looked through the apple trees, all long-lipped and hairy-eared, with alert sideways eyes. The bacchantes forced him to his knees, and thrust a knife next to his shoulder-blade, and whispered 'apologize, apologize' but he would not apologize and called out instead, 'I have seen what I have seen.' A great beefy woman in a leather kilt, her large breasts bare, stood in front of him then, obscuring his view of the throne. She took hold of him by the neck and bent him backwards over her knee, and he could feel his spine crackling. But then, as it burst, he felt a strange turn of consciousness. The nape of his neck which was pressed to the lady wrestler's kneecap now gave him a sensation of nuzzling that kneecap, and a mouth opened there and a tongue came out and he licked the lady's knee. Then his eyes opened in his hair scalp and he could see her great thigh. His legs which were bent backwards began to work again, and he moved them as he felt himself lifted up in the air and placed on the throne with the three ladies. A little blood came from his muzzle, he licked it away with a great tongue. All his senses were incredibly sharp except for his eyes which were blurred, and he flapped hairy lids over them until they grew clearer. Then, with a sudden change of feeling, he found how to see through his sense of smell, how to see through his nostrils, and he turned his head towards the white lady to the right of him and she was all colours, but when he turned to his left there was a partition of the throne, though this also glowed with rainbow colours. Then he knocked at the partition, and the white-black cabin door opened, and the lady who answered it was dark-haired and naked. She had a little wound in the top of her abdomen just below her rib-cage on the right, and she spread it with her fingers and said, look, I have lost my anger, and are your eyes closed, do you not remember me? As he worried who she might be, the cabin dwindled and whirled and turned into some vague lights and a sensation that he was rubbing his eyes, which he found he was, in bed, and the tinny light of dawn was seeping through the curtains. He sniffed, there was something unusual here, his touch of the 'Old American', the autumn catarrh had left him, but as he sniffed again he felt a strange warmth and colour come into his head from the bed where he was lying, and he could smell the metal of the lamp by the bed, and the wood in the impatiently-carved little sideboard with vines and false drawers that stood in the corner. He dressed in an ecstasy of fresh perception, he took a clean shirt from the cellophane wrapper and revelled in the smell of soap and ironing and believed he could see the black skin and worried eyes of the woman who had ironed the shirt. His shoes gave him a brandy made of all the miles he had walked in them; a simultaneous memory like a standing wave in which he could see all that past at one glimpse; his greatcoat was new, and its fleece smelt of machinery and America. He opened the door and the sun rising smelt of all the countries and people it had travelled since the first time the earth appeared in the sky, and he realized he had been standing in the open door knowing and experiencing the bloody history of the world and the glad history of the world for many hours, for the sun was now at zenith. He turned and ran back into the house, looking into drawers for cotton wool, and each piece of furniture he looked in smelt of the forest in which it had grown and of the machinery that had felled it and of the men who drove that machinery. He found the wool and pressed it to his nose, intending to make plugs that would cut down the glare of experience a little, but he could smell the great warehouse the wool had been stored in for several years, he smelt its inventory and its size. With an inspiration he took a candle from its stand and broke off a lump of wax and warmed it in his fingers and made a plug of it, but the wax was so ancient and came from so deep in the earth so long ago that he felt suffocated by the layers of rock and dead forests. In his pocket he found a muffler that had a friendly smell to it, and he wrapped this round his face, and the friendly smell of sheep that lived together in their field of grass and wanted nothing more, came to him, and this was not too much. In time, he thought, as he left the house walking towards the woods whose past he had always conjectured, where the Indian burial ground had been (and the great chiefs were still there to his senses, in the air that filtered through his scarf) I can loosen this cloth on my face, and come into my own. I believe I shall not be like the last man on earth, with every shop open to him and every place to visit, but lonely; for these smells are so loud and alive that I shall have to find a new word — 'smell' is too undetailed — for them, and they are surely persons, with whom I shall learn to converse, and until then I shall be like a child at a party, or like a child at school, or like one in the presence of the adults of time.

His girlfriend was not due to arrive until that evening, and he had wondered whether he would by then be able to match her life of smell as they joined together.

* * *

The squad car sidled to a halt / screeched to a standstill, with the effect of a pounce / beside the walking figure in the high-heeled shoes and the mackintosh. The policeman / the electric mechanism / rolled the left hand / right hand window down, and the peaked cap / bare tousled head / of the policeman, poked out. 'Excuse me, madam / say, lady,' he said politely / brusquely, 'might I ask why you are out on the streets so late at night? / you're crazy to be out on the streets this late / we' re sure there's no trouble but we like to keep our eyes open / Jeeze, there was a rape and a mugging four blocks away this time last week.' The blue-clad / tan-clad / officer / cop opened the door and stepped out of / levered himself out of /the squad car. 'I wonder whether you would show me what you have in your case / Open the case.' 'There's nothing in the case, Officer, but I do need your help.' 'Just open it, please, Madam /I'll just take a look.' And both officers take the suitcase quite gently from the lady in the high heels and the mackintosh and, muttering surprise at its lightness, lay it down on the pavement / sidewalk. It is locked. 'Might I have the key Madam? / I said, open it.' 'But officer,' she said to the four policemen, for the driver had now stepped out of / levered himself through / the right hand / left hand door, 'I told you there was nothing inside.' 'We'll be the judge of that', said all four officers simultaneously on both sides of the Atlantic, two at six o'clock in the morning, and two at one o'clock the same morning, 'Just open the case.' 'Well, actually, there is something in it,' said the lady, 'Indeed / Yeah' said the interviewing officer icily / resignedly. 'I have my transport in this case.' 'Just open the case.' Inside the case were layers and layers of green and white crepe paper arranged in wavy bandages around a superb model of an ocean liner complete in every detail, and done in some very light hard metal. The officer picked it up with admiration / admiration and as he did so a snatch of music came from it. 'Have you a licence for this transistor, Madam /Very, *very* cute, my kid'd love this. Did you make it' / looking coldly ahead / turning to the driver. 'No licence is required, officer / Yes, I made it / It is my soul.' At this the four policemen looked closely at the woman, they had noticed from the first that her dress, if she wore any, was too short and did not show under the hem of her mackintosh / rain-proof topcoat. They had put her down for some raver / hophead trotting home after a party, and it was quite likely that her clothes and whatever she doped were in that case. 'Officer, I need your help. Will you give me your advice?' She parted her raincoat. 'This wound on my side, do you think it is dangerous, do you think I should find a hospital? It stopped bleeding on the ship, and only pained me at first. Is there a doctor who would see me?' A noise like the sea and the throbbing of engines filled the street, and they saw the woman naked under her coat smiling and holding her wound open through a mist. They felt for / their truncheons / loosened their revolvers, and there was a shuddering underground as though a small earthquake passed under their feet, but the street was empty and the pavement-sidewalk unoccupied except for themselves and a few small strips of crepe paper soaked with water. The interviewing officer prodded at these with his boot / delicately lifted a strip with the barrel of his revolver, touched it with a finger which he put to his lips, !!!!!!!!!' / I want to get this analysed, but I'd rather not report. O.K.?' The policemen got huffily into their black car / casually into their tan-and-white car / and accelerated away with their headlights blazing as if to search the empty street and light it like day.

* * *

'Did you not ask for this blood sisterhood? Is the Moon not a door? You come to me with your hair set tight in a bun, your chin in a scowl, your face's skin looking harsh as pale emery. Why, S,' I say, 'have you come looking at me like that, so disapprovingly?' 'You are rotten to women.' 'But I, I never knew you.' 'That's what I mean.'

The pile of scree shifts a little further down, the ghost impends in the tip of my pen's nib, the ink has grown silvery, the paper rough as emery. 'Why, S, who is that large red man you have brought with you, who stands as though introducing you, and apologizing for what you did.' 'It was a cry to him it is my Red Man. He should have been my spirit guide in life, now we are in this place together, where you sit bolt upright in bed frightened of me only because I am no longer flesh and blood. We have to stay here until I can understand what you did, and you can understand me. And the Red Man has been truly dead, but now he aches to return to the dead, and I hope to see those happy lands again, and to wear the face I wore before my parents met.'

The Indian burial grounds where the chiefs and braves dust away like pollen. Or like pemmican in the beaks of birds. It is air-burial, and dead people in their regalia are placed on wooden platforms to evaporate and leave nothing behind, not even bones. They are very holy places, since they are where the ancestors have their being in the great time, which is where there is no time.

Time started when we were born, held up to our mothers' ears like a 'fat gold watch', and ends when we die, praises be. To take the watch out of the wound is to live and be in time, but not of it.

The great Chiefs are relaxed and their pleasure is to do as the birds do, or the tiny crawling lice, or those that build the great pockets of silvery gossamer in the trees, the communal moths who spin and net their homes with mouths that do not ache with lying. The Chiefs are air-fishermen who use their whole selves as baits to catch a fresh life in death, who make themselves a playground for the rich children of nature, they are busy perfecting themselves in these high plazas, these hammocks, busy preparing guidance for English spiritualists. The first officer of the great black-on-white liner *SS Messenger* leant out over the misty sea. The ship was proceeding at full speed since no sea-traffic was reported and none showed on the radar-scope. He was very surprised to see the glaring eyes of a great bird and its outstretched wings appear in the mist at the sea-surface, gliding along, it was unlike any sea-bird he had ever seen, then he saw that it was the figure-head on the prow of a great war-canoe that was being paddled along faster than the liner could go by a row of Red Indians in full feather-head-dress who gravely saluted him as they overtook the ship. 'How!' Later the first officer told the ship's doctor, who said he had seen much stranger things at sea. Perhaps, he thought, they were a consignment of Indian guides proceeding to the English Spiritualist churches for their assignments. The first officer guffawed, palely. But the ship's doctor said: 'You mustn't mock. I am a spiritualist myself. Though that's no reason not to mock. I'm going to tell you something now that I've never told anybody else outside my church. Every evening at six o'clock regularly, ship's time, I talk to my dead wife. She tells me all that has been going on in the spirit world, and I tell her what has been happening down here. She was particularly interested, shocked even out of her customary calm (dead people are often very calm, it seems so to us, at any rate) when I told her about our murder. The thing that surprised her was that there were none of the usual spirit-helpers around, that is, people recently-dead who have taken to the spirit world very intelligently — some people will not believe they are dead when they arrive on the Other Side — and are therefore very good at guidance and counsel when younger spirits arrive. Moreover, though the dead were expecting a young soul to emerge, probably in considerable distress from the murdered body, in fact no soul emerged from the body, and for all they know is there still. This, they said, was very unusual. If a soul remains in the body, they said, for a long time after death, it means either that the soul has been trapped by a very bad karma indeed and is compelled to watch in microscopic detail the disintegration of its earthly habitation; or that the person is a very great soul indeed, who needs this knowledge of matter for some great work. However, to return to your vision, you can see why I am not as surprised as you are, and in fact I would have been very delighted to see such a vision. Beautiful in itself, all done according to the old ways, and auguring well for our country, since the Indian wisdom was precisely directed to survive the death-trauma with intelligence and memory quite intact, so that they could assist others to cross and recross this threshold (as we must) without fear and without forgetting what we have learned in our lives, so that we can bring it to the other world, and receive their knowledge in this. This is why the Red Indian so often becomes a spirit-medium's guide and friend - in that profession you need somebody strong — and that is why they were paddling with superhuman speed over the ocean with the full co-operation of the powers of wind and weather, mediated to them by their guide, a picture of the air's spirit, the great thunderbird, at their prow.'

So the great Red Indian Chiefs make themselves intelligible phantoms, enlarging themselves by entering into the small things. We watched a small spider, beady-red, glossy, hunting among the enormous stone built into slabs on the river's bridge's parapet. It careered over the pocked stone as though there were a castor-wheel at the tip of each glossy leg, as if it were a dining-trolley racing between shell-holes; some grim grey-masked aphid hugged the grey stone tight and our spider collided into it, recoiled from its grimy waxes and joyless stare, and careened away. They practise speaking with their mouthpieces, by the scraping together of horny legs or horny lips until they know the language, until they can speak by the scraping together of the edges of dust, the fractured glass of dust vibrated by the sun's rays. I have scraped a dead Indian from under my nail, in the daylight he looked like a grey smear on a tissue, and I had no idea he would come to me at night, red man of poor S, and rescue me from her disapproval by kind and powerful suggestions.

Thrushes steal the knuckle-bones.
We are moved apart slowly, like chess-pieces.
I daresay hair rises to thatch some nest.
I trust only it relishes the spacious high branches.
But it never cried at its clipping!

Insentient, I fear, that's the pity.
What a beauty if our parts
Studied their pleasures everywhere,
Reported back to our resting ghosts.
That would be earthly bliss!
Pumped up grass-boles, jumped high into tree-tips,
To brood over the cloudy flask of the spider's egg.
The ocean's lens for astrology.

Insentient, I fear. The tippet of foam
Swashed across beaches is more likely to be it,
A soft crackle of bubbles and a dry track
Than the silver-tailed mermaid walking with princes.
Perhaps it is best
To sweeten the buttercups and stouten the turf,
To simmer off bones like a sleep-sweat
Than to give my malison or blessing any reign,
Wars in heaven, the thunderhulk my surprised eyebrows
And the lake swirling, my heel-taps.

(O, but conscious weather!
As I plunge downwards, my crystal lenses
Like a flight of glass bees humming my errands,
Returning to earth, honeycombed with senses,
To meet me again, as I am below.)

But then a new voice broke in. 'Are you still here, Chief Looking-Glass? And S, why, you look so drab and cross. Are you still angry? Look, I have given away my anger, my devilish gall. My lover thought me too cross, and gave me this wound, which released me. You must accept your wound, S, your blood-sisterhood. Allow your soul to travel like a moon, until it learns moon-things, and the shedding of blood is no longer a curse, but a joy, as it is for me. I can shed blood whenever I please, come, Red Chief, taste of my blood (he falls to his knees and puts his lips to the girl's wound). Come S, find your release in this sweet action.'

I am startled by comparisons.
Ice melts from the thatches with the bare restraint
With which the flesh disquantities.
The sound of it beats back like small hearts in sheer spaces.
Stars lie in pools black as pupils
That return their stare, ice-irised. Though nearby
Fire thaws out the greenwood, slow explosion
Of smoke lifts through the chimney, here
My slow trudge snaps snow-crust and prints white darkly;
Blanched breath trudges across the night-sky.
Things shiver and my breath is negatived;
In spread hand I hold the pane.

I slam the door. The brazier sucks
And glows in storeys.
I have the hair, the wax, a specimen of writing,
A pane of ice from the flooded churchyard.
I cast them in, they begin to wreck
And flicker with thin films, a gold stain spreads.
What do I think will happen, but steam and smoke?

I utter the words of vertigo, were I so strong
I should vomit as I spoke them, as some are said to,
Vomit as a thorough utterance. I am unsuitable,
But I will lend it blood.

The great book opens of its own accord,
Its snow-light floods the room, it comes, it comes,
The past has ripped away, there is a thin snow curling
And recurling over jagged shafts
Of reserved lightning, I see boiling tears
And a puckered mouth shouting silence so I razor,
The bowl fills and I grow colder
And the squalling bends to sip. I will not speak in terror
For the looks of terror terrify the dead
To look so terrible, so I've studied calm,
Studied quietness till the right time comes
Which gives me calm. I am magic, then:

Magic enough to greet a person from the scraps and bones
Someone risen out of the feast of coals, a person
Fallen through our festering death, but risen up
And singing gladly of her current death.

'Madam,' says the ship's doctor, 'why do you appear to us in this form? As a murdered person, bleeding to death from internal haemorrhage and a missing gall-bladder, wounded in the liver as Prometheus was, his fiery anger feeding on him in the likeness of an eagle, you have given your anger away, and no doubt it destroys the villain robber elsewhere. The grotesquery (if I may with deferential usage and humbleness employ the expression) of this avatar, the murdered woman with time ticking in her blood, naked, wounded, defenceless, this recalls the religion we have had for so long, which frightens us and comforts few. Why do you have to appear in a manner which quotes at all from Him, can you not come in your own triumphal Car?' 'Dear Doctor, your ship is my Car. It is your species' last chance; I am working through these forms but they are so encrusted with your own defences. Your shows and your lust for power and control, your vulgar nipping cocktails, your bar mirrors and ballroom dancing, your lotteries and ship's games on the promenade deck: I can break out in whatever forms may be strange enough to pierce your defences, your defences which soon make grotesquery of my mysteries. I take a scrap here and a scrap there, a face from poor S, and a hue from the Red Indian, a dish from the grill-room on the quarter-deck, the sensations of a sunbather; pressing on your ways with my being, until perhaps the whole rotten and silly facade will break away and you will enter your birthright. But you have learned so many ways to turn away from me, so many amusing games to close in my face like gates of fantastic wrought iron. You may lose me even after this voyage. You have tried to lose me ever since I was with Jesus in the desert, and he chose not to turn my stones into bread, even though there could be food on this earth for all my children. This earth, if you knew me, you could not pollute with the waste of your industries and wars: your defence programme. I was with Jesus in the resurrection garden, when he told me not to touch him. It was his defence programme, since touch is one of my great gifts, touch and the thinking skin. I was the horned Devil; it was part of your defence programme to clap the horns of my womb on the head of a devil, and to say that we all came from the great father in the sky, and had been found under gooseberry bushes. Whose is that little cottage in the woods, behind the thicket of wild gooseberry bushes? Where is God, Chief Looking-Glass?' (The Chief points seriously at the mountains, then at the sun. He stoops, and cupping his hands, dedicates water from the lake first to the Lady's belly, then to the sun. He offers the water to the Lady, who smilingly drinks it.) 'The horns of sweet generation were fastened above my countenance, and its complexion was darkened with the fierce blood of my womb: it was the defence programme. I was the hell of red flames burning men who had shed the blood of other men instead of honouring mine; that fire is the fruitful lust which blood arouses, and which can only be assuaged by loving me as I bleed. I am the Prince of Darkness: it is your darkness and you cannot see that I am the Princess in it. You reflect me everywhere in your defences: you film me lovingly as Count Dracula, and your blows to my speaking mouth have put the blood there, the curving moon-teeth there, white in the gore, and I have three white wives. I have been the dead men of the quest in the spy movies of your defence programme: I have stared at you from the third bullet-eye shot between the brows of the great villain. You will not look through this eye, and yet you yearn for it, it is my pine-thyrsis, my pine-al, the glowing stone over the well within which the dead people who are the secretaries of the long memory, the white wake of spaceship earth, rise and descend . . . Now I am this Ship, and I appear to the voyagers in matter and time as they have capacity to see me, as they have the desire to see me. For most of you it is as a harmless murdered woman, a figment from a detective story, safely dead . . .' 'You come from inward, then, as much as from outside us?' asks the ship's doctor. 'I am your deepest self.' 'Do the dead truly live?' 'Yes, in you. Earth looks with earth at earth, earth on earth speaks to earth, earth walks on earth to earth . . .'

The Lady now sings:

'Erth owt of erth is wonderly wrought,
Erth hath goten upon erth a dygnite of nowght,
Erth upon erth hath set all his thowt,
How that erth upon erth myght be hye brought.
Erth upon erth wold be a kyng,
But how that erth shall to erth, he thynkith no thyng;
When erth biddith erth his rentes home bryng,
Then shall erth for erth have a hard partyng.

Erth upon erth wynneth castlles and towres,
Then seyth erth unto erth: "This is all owres";
But when erth upon erth hath bilded his bowres,
Than shall erth for erth suff re hard showres.

E rth upon erth hath welth upon molde,
Erth goth upon erth glydryng all in golde,
Like as he unto erth neuer torn shuld;
And yet shal erth unto erth sooner than he wold.'

* * *

'We have a real Red Indian Chief on board', said the social secretary to the cruise director. 'How do you know, did you see his wampum? Did he do his war-dance after drinking all the firewater in the bar? Does he wear at all times an old felt homburg and moccasins? Do his squaws with his papooses bumping their noses on their backs help him make rain-dance on the ballroom floor? How do you know, Gladys, that he is a real Red Indian Chief, and that he is not made of wood, and advertising tobacco? What's his name, and more important, is he a first-class passenger?' 'His name is Chief Bright Glass, but he is travelling under the name of Smith-Jones. Wallace C. Smith-Jones. He is that fat, sunburnt middle-aged man who is always walking on the promenade deck with Dr Saltways. He is travelling incognito because there's no point in his doing otherwise as the title is defunct, but he is very rich because there is oil on the reservation.' 'Hadn't you better invite him to the Captain's Cabin in one of the VIP groups?' 'That's exactly my point.' 'Oh, right. What was he doing in Europe?' 'Studying the white man's religious art.'

* * *

The goddesses of the corn-patch on the road behind the last of the campus buildings were three stooks of corn-fronds. The corn-cobs had been harvested and the earth made bare, relieved of its fruit, put to rest for the winter. It would not do, though, to leave it unattended and without tribute. Accordingly, some of the fronds of the corn-plants had been swathed together, to make three standing green stooks, and positioned in a random but powerful manner on the small field. This corn patch was near, but did not belong to, a small white-painted house of clapboard, in whose porch an apparatus of glass chimes sung day and night in the breeze.

It was the custom of the farmers to pile up these corn-goddesses in each harvested field, to remind the earth of its fertility during the long winter of snow. Red pumpkins were placed at the feet of the teepee-like structures in preparation for Halloween, or

Samhain, the end of the summer, Harvest Festival, feast of the Dead that rest and are consumed in the form of the earth's fruits. The Professor never passed these goddesses without removing his hat in respect. On one of his walks after class he was mildly surprised to see a figure approaching him that also removed its hat as it neared the corn-patch. As it got closer, the Professor saw that it was the Poet. As they passed on the road they courteously waggled eyebrows at each other, but did not speak. Each realized that it was too late for easy conversation now, as they had already travelled two-and-a-half thousand miles on the same boat without exchanging a word.

The goddesses had great strength and presence in the little field, and their leaves at first remained plump and green. As they grew yellower and withered against each other in the colder weather it was as though they sung a diminishing but still audible song while their colour grew less contrasted with the brown earth. On October 20th the first snow fell to settle for a few hours. The white-thatched teepees huddled down in the field: the snow was light and the earth still warm, so they were picked out by the snow which the earth melted but they did not, like tents of paper or motionless ghosts in the field. After the winter snows had laid heavily upon them, then spring revealed their darkened traces, like the few charred sticks of a bonfire. They retained their worshipful feeling, like objects of an open-air church, which they hallowed, as if the corn-spirit itself had directed that they be left there by means of some indescribably holy scripture that opened and closed in men's and women's minds as the seasons changed, and caused them to leave signs and souvenirs of the departed presences, whose return was always expected and hoped for, and never failed.

* * *

The old psychologist with the great freckles on his face was dancing with a famous ballerina, they were dancing the paso doble on one of the first-class dance floors. Suddenly there was an enormous hooting from above their heads which made them clap their hands to their ears. Then an urgent voice came hallooing from the loudspeaker 'Man Overboard, Man Overboard', followed by a brusque request to the passengers not to rush out on the deck, since that would impede the rescue operations. They stopped dancing and sat watching outward through the lounge windows. A waiter stepped forward and asked them whether they would like a drink: both asked for a juice, which shortly arrived, elaborately garnished with fruit slices and jingling with ice. A maroon rose tracer-like over the sea and burst with a bright light and a shower of sparks. The ship's whistle had long ceased blowing; they heard the pounding of feet along the deck as the crew ran for its rescue stations. They imagined that one set of crew would be scanning every inch of the night sea with binoculars for some glimpse of white, a face or a shirt, that would enable them to lower a boat in that direction. The ship's screws had reversed, there was a terrible straining throughout the fabric of the ship — the *SS Messenger* at that moment seemed no more substantial than some nailed-together garden-shed in a high wind, since creaking moved like dream-speech along every corner and cranny wherever the fabric of it fastened together. They saw through their window one of the great lifeboats lowering past, slowly and smoothly. The ship was now totally still, the engines silent, and all the noises outside noises; they felt cut off from this activity in which they could play no part, for they had been informed that the crew were fully-trained and passengers would only get in the way. Gone was the jovial and playful pretence of a passenger merely being crew living in a different part of the ship and dressed differently for fun; there were now two sets of people, one who knew their trade, and one who were cargo and freight, that should be lashed down so that it would not shift in an emergency. The old psychologist sitting with the ballerina watched the lifeboat sliding past their window. 'Look!' she said and pointed to a window further along the lounge. Past this window also a lifeboat slid as it was lowered, past every window the white lifeboats slid against the dark.

Lowering so many lifeboats meant that the search was now desperate, and nothing had been glimpsed, so that the dark sea would have to be quartered. They decided to go along to the aft lounge which was nearest the stern of the ship to see whether the events were clearer down there.

Other people had the same idea, a great many passengers had gathered in the little red lounge to look out over the 'blunt end' of the ship, where a great deal of crew activity was in progress. The most striking change was that the great boiling wake of the ship had gone, for the screws were not turning. Now they felt absolutely surrounded by the ocean, there was no mark of their road here, and consequently of their road back, they were with their camerados on a luxurious raft, crowded and dependent on each other. A pulley had been erected over the stern, and a man was being lowered into the still waters over the screw. Saltways had seen a picture of the *Messenger's* screws once, they were the size of the west end of a cathedral, the little man photographed touching the still blades could have as it were processed spirally to the screw's centre as though he were burrowing into church, and the church towered above him. They looked like the great west window of Salisbury Cathedral, the tallest church in England. The ballerina imagined the little man lowered past these enormous murky blades, like one exploring with his lantern *la cathédrale engloutie* and she paced out a few steps on the red carpet.

They went back to their table in the first-class lounge. The windows were now vacant and dark with night. Occasionally the finger of a searchlight swept out on to the waves. The waiter came forward again and asked whether they would like something more. 'Would you like some hot chocolate?' he said to his companion. They agreed that it was time for their chocolate. It arrived on snowy napkins in thin glasses held by twining silver frameworks. The man seemed preoccupied as he served them. He topped up their dark foamy glasses from a thick jug, and a few drops of chocolate fell on the snowy cloth. He apologized, and made a few quick ineffectual gestures of wiping up, merely smearing the wet black stains, quite unlike the usual style of a waiter in the first-class areas. The psychologist saw that he was frightened and probably the only waiter left on duty now that all the rescue stations were manned, and he decided to seize his chance. 'Was that your friend who went overboard?' he said suddenly and sharply. He had no knowledge of the waiter's friends, and indeed did not remember seeing the waiter before that evening, but experience had taught him that a swift question that assumes knowledge is a way to secrets. 'Mmmmmy friend, Sir, no, it was the murderer . . .' 'What murderer?' snapped the older man. 'I'm sorry, Sir,' said the waiter, and walked quickly away.

For the first time since the serious illness he had had in his thirties, the psychologist waiting for sleep in his first-class cabin (as big as a good hotel-room, and with no trace of seafaring in its appointments), felt like a child put to bed among the goings-on of some adult emergency. The footsteps and the hurryings went on through the night, and there were block-and-tackle noises and the searchlight going when he woke up at dawn. When the steward brought his tea the sun was well up. The ship's engines had resumed their accustomed note, their throbbing like the sound within one's body of life. Without the engines, the ship had seemed like a mere shell, a floating mausoleum dedicated to corpses and funerary matters, a floating city of the dead. Now the living people were once more in procession across the waves in the jovial ship, all flags flying. 'Did they make a rescue?' he asked the steward as he rearranged his pillows to help him sit up for his tea. 'No, Sir, nothing was found,' said the steward sombrely — but he was always sombre, this meant nothing, but merely suited first-class occasions. 'I suppose they have checked the passenger list?' 'Yes, Sir, I understand it was a young man in the tourist class. Very sad.' 'Indeed, I suppose the relatives will be informed by radio . . .' then he stopped suddenly. He had remembered a dream he had during the uneasy small hours of last night. The ship had been full of hurrying footsteps, but no people were visible. He wandered among these invisible crowds until he came within sight of the stern of the ship. The black sea stretched behind them, and there was no wake, the engines had been stopped. On the aft deck where the tennis was played, he saw on the clear space two people embracing, a man and a woman. They broke off their embrace, they seemed happy, but it was as at a temporary parting. The man walked to the stern rail, and the woman waved to him as he vaulted over into the black water. As soon as he touched the surface it closed over his head and he disappeared. Suddenly the band struck up in the ballroom, and the engines started again, and the owners of all the footsteps winked into view, everybody was carrying masks, as at a fancy-dress ball. Once more the great wake stretched out from the ship's end, white and coiling. The ship itself seemed to slip away from the dreamer, leaving him suspended over the creamy wake which coiled away over the smooth water and slowly faded, as if drawn away down below the waves. And then he was below the waves, and the body of the drowned man, whole and entire, had increased enormously as though it could fill the whole sea. With closed eyes the dead man was hauling on a long creamy cord, which the dreamer recognized as the wake of the vessel, and as he hauled he grew smaller, and drew himself with the aid of the cord towards the shore. The dreamer knew that he would eventually haul himself to land, and break the water and walk out on to some beach, but whether it was a beach on the new world or the old, the dreamer could not tell, but he knew he would then be a living man again, and able to take up his life once more, though now he would understand his kinship with the sea, from which all life has come.

The little psychologist got up out of bed and went over to the dressing table mirror. He wanted to write his dream down, as he always did, while it was fresh, because he knew that although it was rarely possible to interpret one's own dreams satisfactorily, the dream remembered would nevertheless affect conduct during the day. He would offer it to a patient for analysis, to help equalize the treatment, democratize it.

He wrote the dream down. How deep it went and how far his understanding could go with it he could not tell. What was immediately apparent was that it called to his first work and pre-occupation in science. He had wished to render the baby conscious in the womb, or the neonate conscious of its former life. As a young man, he had dabbled in spiritualism, and he had become aware of the great semi-permeable barrier between life and death, through which came such strange echoes; which distorted, or seemed to distort, the forces that attempted to penetrate it. He worried about the death-trauma, which seemed as absolute an amnesia as the birth-trauma. But babies were born alive, otherwise we should not be here, their hearts were beating and their healing and growing powers were intact, and these seemed to him like the healing and growing powers that had formed the baby in the womb. So some definite knowledge survived the birth-trauma, but nothing suitable for the laboratory seemed to survive the death-trauma. So he turned his attention to the former. After all, the material of the dead people went into the great womb of nature, just as the drowned man (very likely minced into pieces by the enormous torque of the cathedral-sized propulsion screws, wrenched into pieces before he could take his first lungful of water by the power that drove them from the old world to the new) was even now dissolving in the sea. Had his molecules been able to speak, some newborn child could have given news of his travels from those parts of him that had reached a new womb through the clouds and the rain and the plants and the salads that the pregnant mother insisted on eating, probably because the dead man called to her from the leaf, 'Come, it is time to see again and to touch and smell again, give me life.' So when Saltways became middle-aged, and a psychologist, he had studied all the evidence he could find for recollection in the womb: he would study the dead not as they left this world, but as they entered it. He listened to patients under hypnotism or drugs describing the circumstances of their own birth, recalling sights and sounds as they came into the brilliant clashing world and experienced light for the first time since (on this hypothesis) their last deaths; light and the breathing of air. Even further back, floating in a void and watching the stars, watching the great pulsation from a red sun of warm radiation, waiting for an event like falling into the screws of a liner, the spiral passage down the womb. And earlier still, but these were more difficult, memories of animal life, or fantasies of them, of running like a horse, of gliding like a snake among the feet of wise persons who conversed beyond the grave. And once upon a time in this timeless land where past and future seemed mixed and all knowledge and experience seemed possible, in this place the memories of which, the psychologist began to see, *were* what living men called the Unconscious, a dead person spoke through a patient's mouth. This patient spoke as a young woman who was to be a poet in the future, and die by her own hand. She spoke of the future as though it were the past. She wandered unhappily through the only objects and events she could remember, predicting her miserable life as a prodigy, and her poetry. The psychologist had been able to write down some of the verses his patient mumbled, heard through the coiling recollections and hypnotic fevers of memory, but could not persuade that patient that he was the poet, nor to acknowledge these verses as his own. Then one day many years later the old man with the freckles of age read in the Sunday newspaper a tribute to a woman poet who had just killed herself, and read there the very same verses that he had taken down from his patient wandering through the unborn state, the Bardo, before that unhappy young woman had been born. The notes were properly dated and in situ with the rest of the case history. But case histories were confidential, and the mediumistic patient still alive, so the satisfaction of proof came to him privately.

His experiments went on. He was able to join a clinic in which the mothers had agreed to don a light steel framework that fitted around their bodies and plugged into a reversed vacuum-cleaner motor, so that when the motor was turned on, the air-pressure around their bellies, and thus the air-pressure on the babies growing within them, was reduced. The theory was that this uncollapsed certain blood-vessels in the foetus, so that growing points in the nervous system could be more richly supplied with blood. When the babies were born, they spoke sooner than other children, and showed in their infancies great talents for symbolic expression, in mathematics and the arts. He supposed this showed that they had experienced less damage, through more consciousness of, the birth-trauma; indeed he had visions of these prodigious babies waiting for the right moment and plunging between the contracting fibres and waves of labour so that they emerged like skilful swimmers through rapids, or like a man negotiating the vortices of the screw of an ocean liner. He supposed there must be many of these children walking the world now as young adults. Another doctor too had found similar effects by allowing the baby to be born in darkness, and to lie without the cord cut until breathing started, on the warm belly of his mother. In this way the shock on entering the world was much reduced, the child did not face the aggression of lights, noise and clashing instruments as its first experience of the world. Accordingly its first response to this world was not an aggressive cry of overwhelming anger, but instead — sheer pleasure Once again the passage from the one world to the other had not been overwhelming, and the child had kept some memory of great kindness of the flesh that grew it and ministered to it, and some memory of the events in the womb, perhaps, the nine billion years of evolution recapitulated in nine months. Once again, these children became adept at the arts, at symbolic representation, and they were often dauntingly intuitive. As yet, however, he had encountered no wisdom from beyond the grave from any identifiable sage of the past issuing via the lips of an infant, though these children were so bright that learning appeared to the observer more like a recollection of something they had known before. And what were 'identifiable sages' anyway but constructs of time out of the womb and the tomb, people with long white beards and evident mannerisms. Perhaps the veridical communications he was looking for to confirm his ideas in the world's eyes were in fact irrelevant before the tremendous project of bringing such people as he had observed in infancy into the world, young heroes who had made the journey across these dark thresholds so many times that they became quicker and quicker in their recollections, by a geometrical accumulation. Soon they would be able to teach themselves, and then teach themselves in the womb through the eyes of the mother, like so many ship's portholes and ship's libraries and dancing classes in the first-class ballroom, that they would emerge ready to form a new world. But listening as he had to the strange quests and adventures of people regressed into this world of the unconscious and to the world before birth, he thought that whatever happened would seem like non-ordinary reality, and the annunciations of religion rather than those of a science. And its first catalytic manifestations might very well happen by some such process as was occurring him now, in the eightieth year of his age in this steam-ship, so like a voyage in some womb, that all those memories of his own personal quest had become thus energized, by a dream.

* * *

'. . . *When they made their barks of papyrus they were continuing the lotus into the boat* which was lotus-shaped at prow and stern . . . *Baba* is the title of the old genetrix (Typhon); and *Babia* was the Goddess of Karkemish. The *Bab* (or Beb), which modifies into *Bau*, is the opening of the abyss or cavern, void or pit-hole, also called the hole of the tomb and the well; the *Bob*, Arabic, the opening out of which the water wells; *Bebi* Coptic, to flow and overflow. This Bab became the Bahv or void on which the Hebrew dogma of creation was based. It is also the Babylonian and Byblian Bab called the Gate, but which is more comprehensively the opening, the *outrance,* uterus, or abode of life . . . the "Bob" was the sailor's berth on board ship . . . the "Berth" of the unborn child. (The "Bob" is) the mother herself in the Australian, Akkadian, and other languages. It is the woman, the female, in various languages. It is the womb or belly in the Kanyop, *Pipas*; Pepel, *Pobob*; Mbe. *Fuburu; Bowo* or *Bovo,* in Tiribi. In Dutch the *Pop* is the caterpillar's cocoon. The *Beb*, or *Bub*, in Egyptian is the hole, the pit, a primitive type of the berth. In Gaelic the *Beabh* is the tomb; *Bebo* in Tiwi (African); and *Babisi* in Melon, are hells (in the sky). The *Bab* in Assyrian is the Gate, place of outlet, whence Babylon. But the first Bab is the uterus. Then the hole in the ground or berth on board ship.'

GERALD MASSEY
THE NATURAL GENESIS — VOL. I, p. 462.

* * *

'Captain,' said the first mate, running towards his master along the banks of the stream where they had been strolling, 'there is an old man who has fallen overboard.' 'Not that old man with the long white beard! Quick, it will strangle him by its coilings in the waters unless we rescue him quickly. Find his beard in the water and pull him out by it.' 'Useless, Master,' said the first mate, smiling coyly and hanging her head, to the Master of the Vessel, 'he has fallen among the coiling waters of the great waterfall upstream, and these will strangle him if his beard does not.' 'Then we must hurry. Instruct all the stewardesses to strip off and plunge into the boiling-white water, they have no beards and are therefore in no danger, but take care they remove their white uniforms before plunging into the stream, as these will coil about in the water's torsions and strangle them.' So all the ship's crew hurried up to the waterfall, their running footsteps noiseless on the fertile banks, and there they found an old man, wet, and towelling himself vigorously with his long white beard. 'Old man,' they said to him, and the freckles of age had joined together on his face to make a vizard or mask suitable for a fancy-dress ball, 'we thought you were lost, strangled by the strong cable of your beard, or the flowing, plaited cords of the falling water, the terrible vortices like those of a mighty ocean-liner's good cathedral screw.' 'No,' said the old man, 'I am in no danger from the flowing water. What I have practised through my years until today, which is my birthday, is that knowledge which will take me down on a descending vortex, and throw me safely on to the bank on an ascending vortex.' 'Mighty man, will you not teach us that skill?' 'A sailor should not drown,' he replied, 'it is the first knowledge of seamanship. It is inborn knowledge, natal knowledge learnt from the navel, navel knowledge, knowledge of following the cord, which twines from the navel as my long white beard coils from my chin, natation, navis, naves, of the ship, and nautae, nautical, of the sailing-master. You are safe, my Captain, if you are a good seaman, and have good semen, then you know the way.' At that, the old white man lifted the captain of the *SS Messenger*, thirty-five years in the service of the line, from cabin-boy to master of the ship, lifted him with no effort by the scruff of the neck and threw him into the rushing waters, upon which the Captain made a violent effort of twisting his body like a cat in mid-air, and landed once more on the bank, poised on all fours, and this was the way he woke by the side of his berth, on fours, the tangled sheet catching at his foot, in no attitude suitable to the termination of the slumber of such a distinguished seaman, afraid of water.

* * *

It was perhaps fifteen minutes' drive and a further twenty

minutes' walk through the woods from the Glass Cottage to one of the notable beauty spots of Cornwall, St Nectan's Glen and Kieve, or cauldron. A kieve is a circular pot fashioned by water in rock from the endless scouring around of stones, small boulders, branches, and other inclusions brought down in the waterfall. Such cauldrons may be any depth, depending on the circumstances, though it is usual for them to be quite shallow, a couple of feet or so. In Tintagel's rocky valley, which is not far away from St Nectan's, there are many charming kieves in the little waterfalls, a few feet in depth, always boiling white, a few feet across. In due time, which due time is measured by tens of thousands of years, the outer wall of the pot may scour away, rubbed by the water, and the kieve becomes a deep bevelled cleft in the fall. It is usual then for another cavity in the rock to be formed by years of turbulence and the circulation of fragments, out of which the water boils in its motion, and a second kieve is formed. There may be a series of these shelves in the fall to be seen, but usually only one kieve at a time in a fall, since the water must fall directly down to make such an impact on the stone.

The kieves in the Rocky Valley may have been charming; charming was the wrong word for St Nectan's Kieve. The fall itself was perhaps sixty feet high, and fell directly into a perfectly round cauldron which overflowed across flat sheets of rock into the stream running through the woods. These woods were reputedly haunted by three grey ladies. It was claimed that the cauldron itself was some twenty feet deep or more, and the roar of the water had a bass note that suggested depth, echoing round the rocky defile of the cliff through which the water fell. At the head of the cliff was a small dwelling-place with a few tables and chairs on a rough terrace where visitors could refresh themselves. In fact the kieve seemed to be owned by the people here, since there was a wooden door marked 'Waterfall' which had to be unlocked, and a fee paid to them. The small brochure they had printed spoke of the fall's height and the cauldron's depth, how the sound never stopped since the wood was sheltered and the winters warm, and how their house was built on the site of St Nectan's Hermitage where the Cornish Saint had lived and prayed and healed long before modern England existed, long before the

Normans came. There were a few sentences telling of a tradition that St Arthur's Knights were baptized in St Nectan's glen. The fall stood like a full white tree of sound among green mosses.

The proprietor of The Hermitage tea-shop unlocked the peeling door to the waterfall, and cautioned them to mind the steps, which were worn (as by the procession of countless pilgrims) and damp with the air of the glen. They picked their way down carefully, awed as always by the atmosphere of the great beeches that sprung from side to side of the path. The beeches seemed to form eyes and noses in their barks, grimacing expressions of gods and animals. The man's and woman's vision was sharpened by the talk of ghosts, by the physical awesomeness of what they had come to see. They wished to experience it to the full extent of their powers. They did not refuse any vision, even Disney faces in the trees. The path wound down and they came to the sheets of rock over which the stream fast-flowed, and they passed through a thicket of shrubbery. The sound became more and more urgent, and the sight of the fall, thick, bounding white into its basin like the bounty of a white sun falling on its planet, like the white fecundation of a god finding its great vase, stopped them in their tracks. 'May I photograph it?' he whispered, 'I want to use the flash.' Taking pictures of the Falls was known to be difficult, there was such glaring whiteness about the turbulent water in the dusky defile that luck must be on the side of the photographer as well as skill. Eleven o'clock in the morning in summer-time was known to be the best time, because then a shaft of sunlight fell slant-wise on the white energy of the kieve's surface, and the standard postcard picture had been taken at that time. They wanted good pictures for themselves, but it was early autumn, and teatime.

By crossing the stream and standing on the flat rock platform in two inches of water it was possible to point the camera directly up the white spinning shaft of the fall, and to see clearly the twin spouts of water that jetted over the lip of the pot and which crossed over each other like a nerve chiasma or crossed breast-bands before they reached the racking stream below. The drawback to this shot was that the spray splashed the camera lens and blurred the picture even during the short time that it took to adjust the viewfinder. One could snatch shots, and this is what he did, using this time a flash, in the hope of bringing up contrasts on the speeding water. The other shot he needed was of the precise way in which the water entered the kieve. For this he would have to climb up a dwindling pathway that led through the shrubbery on the other side of the fall, to a small ledge. Here, by stretching forward on his belly, he could reach over far enough, he thought, to find his view. 'Please take care,' his companion said. 'You mean where the face floats?' for in the postcard at this point some glare in the leaves and the water had made a fierce bewhiskered face that grinned out of the picture. He climbed without difficulty, though he got his trousers smeared with the fern-mould. Once at the ledge, he saw that his scheme was sound, and he stretched out and leant with the camera, put his eye to it, and found that the impact of the falling column on its own substance would make the picture he needed. From this angle, the water in the pot was keeling round and round in a massive way, with its whole volume, but there was a further structure of more lightly etched vortices on the bubbling surface. He thought that the whole system moved clockwise in the basin. He would like a movie camera to make sure of this, but the noise was a bit confusing and there were other motions in the water, one a kind of crosswise tucking in of the surface at one point, which would make the motion, perhaps after one rebound from the insides of the pot, helical. He thought he could detect a twice-round feeling in the motion of the water, as though it coiled within itself a number of times before falling out in the crossed bands over the lip. He had a fancy that it coiled in this manner once, twice, thrice, and then half round and over, but he could not be sure. A cry from below cutting across the hum of the fall warned him that he had been leaning too far over, and he drew back, waving genially at the woman below. There was a smaller ledge which would give him a better view, and it would be best to crawl on to this rather than to step across, since it was a very small ledge, and a little rounded at the edge. The camera round his neck safely on its strap, he inched forward, but something seemed to catch and tug at his ankle and with a cry that the water's sound quenched, he was over the slippery ledge and headfirst into the kieve.

The woman noticed that the rock face was suddenly empty. Her attention had been away from his antics on these invisible ledges, for she had promised herself that she would try not to care. The ledge was empty. Was he on his way down through the shrubbery? She ran towards it, but realized that the path was quite empty. Could he have fallen — fallen into that white torment among the rocks scouring round and round — what could she do — splashing in the stream she ran towards the white bands that she expected to run red at any moment. The water's note seemed to her to have changed to a ruminative sound, like an animal that is digesting. It was all unreal to her, she could not realize that he had fallen and was now at this moment struggling among the white currents of St Nectan's Kieve. Suddenly a glistening thing like a seal flopped over the lip of the pot and fell sprawling in the shallow racing pool there. She saw blood on his scalp and his nose, he was very white, but he was breathing. She pulled at his clothes but could not shift him, and knelt instead in the water to cradle his head and keep his mouth in the air. His eyelids flickered and his eyes opened. To her surprise they smiled, and looked to her kinder than ever before, when he spoke he spoke smiling, though blood was running down over his eye. 'Dearest, I have been on a long journey, though I'm afraid I have brought back no pictures of where I have been to show you,' he touched the wrenched-off top of the camera which still dangled round his neck by the strap. 'Here, let me . . . can you crawl a bit out of this water?' They were both completely drenched, 'I don't want your head falling back into St Nectan's water, so if you get on to the bank I'll go and get help.'

Not much later they were sitting by the fire at the hermitage, drinking sweet tea and wrapped in blankets. The people there were very kind and concerned: never during the eighteen years they had been there had such a thing happened, though there were tales of bones rolling round and round in the kieve until they were as small as dice, and they say a clergyman once tried to swim St Nectan's Kieve in the eighteen-eighties but emerged in pieces, and they never found the head. The couple could not themselves ring for a car, since there was no phone, but the proprietress ran to a nearby farm that she said would be glad to drive them down the cattle lane to their car parked at the edge of the main road. At home in the Glass Cottage she said to him, 'Did you see bones dancing in St Nectan's Cauldron?' 'No,' he said, 'I saw a great liner sailing over the ocean. The portholes were human faces. They launched a little boat for me, and gave me a berth. When the liner reached the shore the black and white of it broke up into a great concourse of people, black and white and red, who went their various ways into the land. I had to vault over a little stone fence, and it was then that I hurt myself.' The grazes, for they were no more, were his only injury. 'You must have been very near death, and so was I, for I could not have gone on living if you had died so suddenly and cruelly.' 'I was very near something, but it didn't feel like death.' And he looked at her with that very kind expression which was new to him since he had traversed the Kieve.

* * *

THE WATERFALL OF WINTER

Project for Dave Westby Sculptor —
from the Adirondacks, greeting

The White Worm Falls the White Lady Falls
The Albino Noise swoops over the bloodstone cliff

The sculptor is in love with these Falls
In love with this cliff like beefsteak, with these
Water-lianas and cold smokes smashed,
Or white monkeys chattering in the smoke,
Or as though the slim white dead danced sideways
                through the trees
On a crossing wind.

The sculptor cuts a monument of Merlin in the
                bloodstone cliff,

He swings under the smoky eaves on his drumming
scaffold,
Wet in his shining clothes, the white falls running with
chisel-blood,
He carves the face beardless with salient lips and brows
That catch its water white with foaming beard:

A white beard of cold smoke and a white-sleeved robe
that is alive
Over a blood-red body —
or the white shadow of a woman hovering
Which the red body casts —
or the white lady's body beating,
Which rock-red Merlin haunts . . .

The youthful sculptor plants along this fast brook
All the pharmacopoeia a wise man needs
Should a wise red man come
Blue tobacco, dock, stringent oxalis

Across the steely lake you may see the Falls flashing
Like red gold under white sail

He carves the bloodstone penis
It sets a cunt-current pouting in the smooth pour
In winter it freezes and no longer waves like a woman's;
A man of blood curdles in the white wife of water;
A red man marbled deep in the frosty woman;
In spring-spate over the warm mere the sound of
thunder and enlightenment.

* * *

I boorded the Kings ship: now on the Beake,
Now in the Waste, the Decke, in every Cabyn,
I flam'd amazement, sometime I'ld divide
And burne in many places; on the Topmast,
The Yards and Bore-spritt, would I flame distinctly,
Then meete, and joyne.

* * *

In mid-Atlantic we ran into an electrical storm. One of the officers was making an informal patrol of the promenade deck when he saw a curious appearance about a lifeboat stanchion. Corrosion, perhaps, he would have a rating paint it. As he got closer he saw that it was as though bright flecks were speeding through a blue sheath that wrapped the bracket round, and flowing into the deck. The sheath was a pale blue colour, almost invisible In the early sunlight, like a butane flame, and the flecks were many colours, gold, silver, crimson, turquoise. Unwisely the young officer reached out to touch the phenomenon. There was a loud explosion and he was thrown sprawling, narrowly missing a steel bollard with his head.

Up on the bridge the second officer was making his inspection. In this modern vessel there was still a wheel that nominally controlled the rudder, and a rating now was taking his turn at it. But the wheel controlled the ship within quite narrow limits; when any momentous change of direction was required the great black panel with its winking lights and white dials supervised the alteration of course by computer, taking into account tides, winds, temperature, and other variables before setting the course exactly. Despite this, the wheel still had in it the feel of the ship, and the steering-shafts penetrated through the vessel right down to the stern keel, where the rudder was, and through it came a kind of distillate of the movement of the ship's course and of the energy of its propulsion. Traditionally too, there was a binnacle with a compass, the short column convenient to the wheel so that the steersman could consult the needle to see his exact direction by magnetic north, but once again, this kind of reckoning had become subsidiary to their echo from the communications satellite, two hundred miles overhead, that throughout the entire voyage, was plotting their exact position on the ocean. When the purser gave his pep talk to the passengers to describe the marvellous vessel they were to live in for the next week, one of the points he emphasized was the safety of these new systems. 'We can never be lost, you see,' he said, 'even on what you may think is a featureless waste outside your windows.

We beam a signal up to the satellite, the satellite beams a signal to the computer ashore, which beams back (*it sounds like a jolly party*, beamed an inebriated passenger) to the satellite, which broadcasts a signal that tells us our exact position on the ocean. It could do the same for a much smaller vessel, like a canoe, except that a canoe would not be strong or large enough to carry the necessary equipment.'

Now, halfway through a voyage that had, so far, not been quite routine, the second officer surveyed his bridge with pride. It was a privilege to serve with the most up-to-date and largest ocean liner at present plying this route. He watched the cool efficiency of the machinery, quietly alive in its panels, proof against most human foolery. He watched the steersman, good type of a young merchant seaman, alert and calm at the wheel, standing in a pose immemorially the same since men first sailed the sea and invented the steering rudder and compass. He bent forward to take his bearings by the compass. The card was a blur. He rubbed his eyes and looked round the room, then bent to the card again. It was a blur because it was spinning so fast. 'Here, Jones, whatever your name is, what's this? Don't you take compass bearings?' The man at the wheel did not appear to hear him, his calm nautical face was miles away, flying before the vessel like a stormy petrel, or simply asleep. 'Here, Jones, wake up'. The officer took the seaman by the shoulder, which seemed to snap under his grip and twist away. He staggered and recovered his footing, but could not see the helmsman at first. Then he noticed him crumpled a few feet away, on his face on the floor. The wheel itself was now revolving, slowly at first, but then faster and faster until it became a blur. It was covered with a blue coating of fire that glowed and began to throw off sparks, like a catherine wheel. Fortunately the automatic panel had disengaged the wheel from the rudder at the first moment the mechanism had perceived an irregularity. There was a sudden bang and a hard percussion in the air that stunned him so that he could not see, then all was normal again, except for a sulphurous smell, a stiffness in the second officer's right hand fingers, and the crumpled black heap of the helmsman under the wheel. The officer bent forward over the binnacle and saw that the card was not revolving now, that it had settled down, and that the large northern arrow-marker on it was pointing to the left, quite correctly for the homeward run. Then he realized that they were not on the homeward run, but outward bound for New York, and that North should be on their starboard bow, not on their port.

In the restaurant the head waiter reassured his best client that the *Agneau de Bruxelles* would not be long delayed, and why not open another bottle of the Cliquot while they were waiting — it would alert their taste-buds for the treat in store. As he was talking, a small procession consisting of the two table-waiters, the wine-steward, a silver trolley, and the white-clad head chef, all with serious smiles, approached the table. The head-waiter turning, saw them, and greeted them with flying fingers and a cascade of smiles, and the chef, not to be outdone, lifted the great silver dome covering the dish on the trolley, with a remarkable flourish. There was a delicious odour of meat and sauces in the air, and a small ripple of applause came from the hungry diners. With further flourishes the chef picked up the dish of *Agneau de Bruxelles* ('The only good thing that ever came out of Belgium,' whispered the maitre d' with fawning complicity into the ear of the diner footing the bill for this extraordinary treat) and wafted it under the noses of all who were about to partake. Then he returned it to its trolley, picked up a dark bottle of brandy, and poured a liberal portion into a large spoon fastened into a frame over a lighted spirit-lamp. After a while, the vapour of the brandy caught fire with a pale blue flame; the chef picked up the spoon, and with many theatrical gestures, poured it carefully over the glistening, steaming meat, which as the spirit spread, seemed to burn with a lambent flame. Suddenly it seemed the flame spread where it had no business, and ran off the dish and spread its luminosity over the white cloth and over the silver rails of the trolley, at the four corners of which it burnt upright from the small ornamental pillars there. Soon it covered the trolley. The chef stood aghast, in mid-gesture, his fingers spread out towards his masterpiece from Brussels, which was now luminescing like a set piece in a firework display. Like a contagion the blue flame ran over the table-cloth, and up the white-clad arm of the chef, who was soon coated with it; it ran in streamers from his outstretched fingers. From the trolley it leapt to the waiters, from the table-cloth it leapt to the diners, and there was an indescribable tension, as though the air was about to tear, then tear it did with an almost inaudible ripping sound, and the electric lights flickered out. Still the blue flame raged, the people on whom it raged without injury struck stiff in their astonishment, and table after table now caught until the room was full of flickering blue ghosts of a dining company of people, a 'feasting presence, all of light'. Then a woman screamed and the lights came on.

Nobody was hurt. There was no sign left after the passing of the flame except that everybody felt excited and alert, and had acquired a good appetite, which after several days of rich ship's food, was by no means usual. The maître d' began to insist on the chef's offensive masterpiece being returned to the kitchens, and the chef in his turn was about to retire in a huff, he had crushed his tall hat about his ears, but the man who had ordered *Agneau de Bruxelles* insisted on tasting a piece. With reluctance a piece was placed on a clean plate, sauce was ladled, and he lifted it to his mouth. A dreamy expression came over his face as he chewed. All bent forward, anxious and interested. 'Absolutely, ab-so-lutely I have never . . . a dream . . . ?' he pronounced. 'Please serve the lamb . . .' He took a sip of wine, and a light blue flame almost invisible in the electric light ran from his lips twice around the inside of the glass.

The Professor had been a witness to these events, and participant in them — he too had 'flamed amazement' sitting at his table, spoon halfway to his lips and soup crowded with little yellow-beaked flames. When the lights went on and the dining-room gave its great sigh of astonishment, its release of bated breath (then slowly the tempo of eating picked up, and the clatter and hum of talk resumed as though nothing untoward had happened) the Professor realized that those few minutes were the first time his mind had not been preoccupied with the figure of the murdered woman since that sad event had occurred. It was as though her white wounded body that had taken up apparently permanent residence in his mind, had truly only done so for a period of incubation, and what she was about was to turn into sheer power, or distillate of cognition, a flame that ran its light everywhere and did not consume. Now, instead of the sad corpse, the glamorous meat, he had the blue shadow of a woman in his thoughts that walked and lived and danced quite freely. That, like flame, could assume the form of anything in the world, though it would always return to its resting state as the blue shadow of a woman, and this woman-shadow is standing interested and attentive though without apparent features, only a sometimes profile — just as shadows are, only this one is a flame also, and possibly the flesh of the discarded body had only been the shadow of this versatile energetic reality. He had for some years adopted an expedient for distracting his thoughts from any obsession that had lodged there, of clearing his mind by replacing some preoccupation with an image that was both commodious and precise: he called it his 'softlythundering mirror' and he always kept the means to construct it in his suitcase. These consisted of a long plastic slide such as one slips on to the ends of posters so that they hang straight down — a loop of string is fastened to the slide for attaching to a picture-hook — a large pair of paper-scissors, a roll of sellotape, and a roll of aluminium foil dull silver on the one side, and silvery and polished enough on the other to reflect a recognizable figure, that would shimmer and part and return to the sound of a silvery thunder as the foil shook on a window-breeze or was shaken by hand. Sometimes he called it his 'dry lightning' when it was hung up in the middle of his room, attached to the ceiling or some fixture by means of the tape and the plastic poster-holder, seven foot tall bolt of reflective lightning, lightly thundering. Now the Professor saw that he must take, not just a slab of the foil to hang up, but he must wait until the blue shadow of the dead woman passed again through his mind, and he must allow it to fall on the dull-side of the foil, and he must mark it there with a crayon if it stayed still long enough, and if it didn't he must wait again, and he must cut out the precise shape of the shadow, and he must hang it up to reflect and thunder with the sound of faint cymbals, and be his bright companion when he grew dull.

The theatricals had eaten at the first sitting of dinner, and were busy with their charades for the final night's party. The full word was Aphrodite. They had made large fuzzy-wuzzy wigs for

Afro, and concocted a little demonstration with placards reading 'black power'. They did not think that there were likely to be black power leaders on board who would be offended. For the second syllable they had a comic drunken sailor with painted alcoholic cheeks and a traditional sailorsuit with broad collar and bows, a cardboard accordion and a real bottle, singing a tipsy Negro spiritual sitting on his ditty box. Afroditty. For the Whole they were painting a cardboard shell with waves and they had a little luggage trolley to fasten it to. Aphrodite — one of the girls, boldly topless — would be wheeled in to the strains of 'Rule Britannia' and she was to be given a trident to hold, and allowed to wear her hair down. One of the boys dressed as the Captain of the *Messenger* would kneel to her and recite some especially-written verses beginning: 'Dear Aphrodite, from my vessel fair/I send you greeting with traditional care.' The tableau had been set up on the cinema stage, their performance area, and the quasi-Captain was on his knees and about to recite. 'Quiet, please, everybody,' said the MC, who was one of the crew, 'Right Cap'n, let's hear you!' The Captain began:

> Hail Sovereign Queen of secrets, who hast power
> To call the fiercest Tyrant from his rage;
> And weep unto a Girl; that has the might
> Even with an eye-glance, to choak Marsis Drum
> And turn th'allarm to whispers, that canst make
> A cripple florish with his Crutch, and cure him
> Before Apollo; that may'st force the King
> To be his subjects vassal, and induce
> Stale gravity to daunce . . .

The boy's voice gained in power, and placed as he was half-inclined to his listeners, they could see that his face was working and his eye glinting as he pronounced the words with more fervour than his friends had ever observed in him before on any occasion. Aphrodite in her cardboard shell was looking as though she couldn't believe her ears, and her trident was leaning at an uncommanding angle — it was in fact a spit from the kitchen and they had bated the prongs with slivers of cork.

. . . the pould Batchelor
Whose youth like wanton boys through Bonfires
Have skipt thy flame, at seventy, thou canst catch
And make him to the scorn of his hoarse throat
Abuse young lays of Love; what godlike power
Hast thou not power upon?

'That's rather good,' observed the hard-bitten young MC, a too-handsome blond boy with bright teeth and grey flannels, 'Did he learn it at school, I wonder? I hope he doesn't go on too long.' 'It's lovely, but not part of our charade,' said the young woman with the long grey hair which she had unpinned from her sailor's cap and which now fell in a dully silver cascade, 'what is that blue colour on his head?'

. . . To *Phoebus* thou
Add'st flames, hotter than his the heavenly fires
Did scorch his mortal Son, thine him; the huntress
All moist and cold, some say, began to throw
Her bow away, and sigh: take to thy grace
Me thy vow'd Soldier . . .

The electric lights had flickered and dimmed, and in the low light the boy seemed to be wearing a blue helmet shining with its own light in which flecks of colour streamed, and which palpitated about his head as though a great glowing butterfly had settled there. Behind the figure of Aphrodite too there was an appearance as of dark cloud gathering.

. . . who do bear thy yoak
As 'twere a wreath of Roses, yet is heavier
Than Lead it self, stings more than nettles;
I have never been foul-mouthed against thy Law,
Ne'er reveal'd secret, for I knew non; would not
Had I ken'd all that were

Aphrodite was now listening with great stormy wings spreading behind her back. Globes of fire bounced and scuttled around the stage. Suddenly all coalesced into a great fountain of fire that flew up through the room without making a sound. The lights came on again, and the charaders looked at each other, then the MC ran up on to the stage. 'Are you all right?' 'Yes,' replied the Captain, 'I feel fine. Could you hear what I was saying?' 'Indeed! Was it Shakespeare? Did you learn it at school?' 'I don't know what it was. I simply felt a book had opened in my mind, and I read out of it.'

* * *

Walking through this air was like wearing a very good pair of magnifying spectacles. The trees were on fire with their slow combustions which were like cries and music and vintage; it was as though the usual visual spectrum had been extended by these very clear spectacles of autumn air to the subvisible radiation lying beyond the limit of visible red, and the supervisible lying beyond the violet; but our usual notion of a spectrum is a strip of banded light — here the range of visual melodies were turned and twisted in chord after chord of unexpected, newly-created colour, in orange, beige, lime, umber, teak, fresh green and charring glede all on the same tree like a new statement of that tree's ability to charm and make tree magic, a celebration of the fruit accomplished and a final flaring of ability overflowing from the energies that had overcome the death of winter, like the vibrations of energies passing through the world, the red shift as they passed through into winter and the crystalline secrets of death: great beings dreaming visibly and sweating more spectra of odour to match their colour through change after change of the fire that the world is made of, the fire that is music, in St Nectan's Glen, in the foothills of the Catskill mountains, where a brown-and-green snake switches away into the beige-fruiting grasses.

* * *

'Stars above, stars below; know this, and be happy!'
Hydrogen to helium; burning sunlight, slow H-Bomb.

My tree drinks the light, says Jesus, with its leaves
Sculpting the sugars of this sweet apple
Carpenting the carbon dioxide to hydrogen
Red apple I pluck and devour and digest
The sweet fuel-sugars run through my blood.

As I lift my hands on fire to heal you,
The hydrogen dislimns, says the child Jesus,
From these sugars and they melt to water

Warmth and water, the transactions of hydrogen,
The Bible of God of my Mother's arms,
The water-maker from the stars. Look! I piss
I am the water-maker from the stars

Am I not, it is yellow as sunlight
I twine the sunlight through its beams or the starlight
My mother holding it and showing me how.

* * *

In his tourist-class cabin, the Professor pissed blue fire in the darkened lavatory into a pan filled to the brim with yellow-beaked flames. In a first-class cabin, a noted industrialist ejaculated blue fire into his mistress, who looked down at him from lambent blue irises. She had stopped taking her Pill a month ago without telling him, and she had great hopes of bearing him a son in secret, or a daughter. In the event it was a daughter, and the baby conceived in the last-to-one day of the voyage, was born unblemished, except for a slight red birthmark below her rib cage, high up on her abdomen on the right. This child would travel down the Hudson with all the other passengers at no extra charge, invisibly, microscopically. In the aft tourist lounge twenty people were sitting comfortably as if listening to a concert, they had often so sat listening comfortably to a concert. On this occasion a large potted fern had been placed on the small stage, and it was glowing with many colours, which were passing along its fibril leaves and between its branches like three-dimensional circuitry and a harpsichord playing complex, vigorous and interesting music. A series of perfumes wafted from the plant: smells ranging from hot metal to wet mould. Then the colours passed from the plant all at once, in one sheet, like a flapping ghost made of rainbow passing through the wall. The audience woke out of their trance, 'That was the best film I've ever seen on this voyage,' said one violet-haired dowager to another, reaching her hand out and stroking her friend's cheek. Coruscating globes swam solemnly into the Captain's cabin where he was composing a letter to his lawyer. They clustered together, revolving at speed, and seemed to read the letter over his shoulder. Then one detached itself and passed into his skull with a slight detonation. His pen drooped and fell from his hand. A smile of pleasure grew broadly on his face, and a bulge grew in his trousers. The globes vanished each with a slight, distinct detonation. The captain's smile grew. In the darkened gymnasium the old yoga-teacher practised pranayama, energy-breathing, with two curling tusks of blue firey air flaring from his nostrils as he exhaled. His smiling face radiated content. The chef discovered that his best copper pan was welded to the stove. Then the *SS Messenger* sailed out of the electrical storm and all to whom these marvellous events occurred at that instant started to wonder if they had been dreaming. Even the ship's doctor said to his assistant, who was grinding a new supply of indigestion powder in the large mortar, 'Strange things happen at sea, but people dream stranger dreams than on land.'

The autumn of burning leaves and brown snakes moved over the Catskill foothills like a beneficent lava. He felt like a man of radium walking through the deep circulations of molten rock and fused gems that flowed around the earth's centre, he felt that he saw in this autumn the deepest and first geology from which all this colour flowed, the branching trees in the rock, the slow lightning of silver in the mine, the trunks of darkness that were rivers of metal. He knew that the reactions in the glorious sun that made light for the trees to become visible were the same star-metabolism by which the trees built themselves, their sugars, and their cool furnace colours out of air, water, and that very same light; he had read also that the colour of the first and original rock from which all the surface of the earth and the things on it grew, the rock known as olivine, was green, fresh green, like the sea.

* * *

Venus stood as if nailed to the radar-mast, in full opposition to the sun, whose after-glow could still be seen, as if it were shining from deep within the sea. Slice the night's black apple in half, in your left hand you will have the five-pointed section of that process called Hesperus, star of the evening, in your right hand you will have Lucifer, star of the morning. Both are the same planet, Venus; depending whether you look at it with the light of the rising sun, so its nature changes. 'Bright star! would I were steadfast as thou art,' whistled the ship's doctor as he paced briskly round the boat to a tune of his own composition, 'what a bright blue nail in the sky, thou art, by bugger. Bless thy bright moist ovary, what wavery pictures are passing combed out of the air by that staff or mast to which thou nailest thyself, like Ahab's sovereign, what waverly pictures of mayhem and bomb-awfulness propagated by those whose skeletons do not vibrate in tune, even the mast like a monkey's skeleton that catches these apparitions upon which feed my necessitous colleagues clustered round the daisy-chain television in our fo'castle or wardroom, depending on our braids, is in better vibration than those tortured waves. Ah (as a waft of scented air came out of and over the sea) they are mowing hay on the Andes, Mr Starbuck, so why not join them, this great wave-reaper cannot be so honourable a job. How, with that star shining there and the ocean breathing with such apple-orchard breath can that television aether contain such terrible fantasies and lies without stinking of all the unredeemed dead who are not truly dead for they never lived. With that star vibrating at our mast, dear lady, are you (raising his face to the star) the president of our line? Are you the owner of this Vessel? Proud to give you service, ma'am (his hand in a straight blade at the peak of his cap, very nautical and sincere) but will you forgive an old seadog who loved the boys first and came to Your service late and scarred and corrupted by the desire for a fast buck and a quick fix? (The star nodded and winked, tears sprang to the doctor's eyes.) Aye, thank you ma'am. Your sarvant ma'am. God for England and St Nelson.' And he walked quickly back to the ship's surgery to give himself a fix with a new clean needle properly sterilized.

* * *

The great ocean liner *SS Messenger* in her black-and-white uniform sailed into the mouth of the Hudson River, its wake like a memory in the water reaching back to their starting-point at the English Docks. On the ship's bridge all was activity and purpose, for this was the moment of seamanship's own task: the navigation of the centre of the Verrazano Bridge so that the liner would pass exactly through, leaving both itself and the bridge unscathed. The computer in the sky could not help them with this task.

It was as though the ship's personnel had only been pretending throughout the voyage: the computer had held them in its reins. Now the men came into their own: the appointed helmsman was a ranking officer, and the minute adjustments he made to the course were true adjustments. If he made a mistake, no guiding radio would offer an obliging beam. The vessel would simply crash into the bridge.

Verrazano Bridge, soaring like the arched brow of an eye over the harbour from Staten Island to Brooklyn, was choked with colourful early-morning traffic. Now as the liner approached, the traffic crawled to a standstill, and shirt-sleeved drivers got out and leaned over the parapets to watch. Deliberately as an arrow in its bow, swung on to the target by Its archer, with its green-white wake feathering in the rear, *Messenger* manoeuvred. The accurate centre of their target was the place where mast and funnel would just appear to graze the lower surface of the roadway loaded with the blue, red and green cars, the yellow tankers full of petrol, the freight lorries, the green trucks full of fruit. Far in the distance, to the South, the liner's left hand, the Statue of Liberty stood like a metal giantess, swathed in mist, rearing her cold torch.

The morning silence was like the city holding its breath. Then one of the grubby little tugs that had been clustering round the *Messenger* like worker ants intent on grooming their queen, hooted with her steam-whistle. Before the echo had time to gather from the shores, its companions had followed suit with their whistles in a hooting and fluting that bounced and echoed round the severe walls and hollow warehouses of dockland. Easily and slowly the ship had plumbed its entrance through the arch. Then from the great span rainbowed with vehicles, all the car horns came trumpeting in greeting and affectionate derision, as the liner's sharp end entered like a clean needle slipping into a vein; the yearned-for fix. The American Connection was achieved. 'A beautiful insertion,' crowed the first officer, bent over his dials.

* * *

www.ingramcontent.com/pod-product-compliance
Lightning Source LLC
LaVergne TN
LVHW091001080826
845145LV00003B/1078

* 9 7 8 1 9 0 5 0 2 4 1 0 0 *